After being kicked out of his parents' home at the age of fifteen due to being gay, Tony Harsnen always felt grateful that his older brother, Jerome, took him in. That's what had urged him to work uber hard to make his own way. The last thing he wants to do is run back to his brother when he has a problem. Unfortunately, Tony has to put his pride aside for the needs of a friend.

When Tony helps his best friend, Shellie, escape her abusive ex-husband, he should have known that wouldn't be the end of it. After the controlling bastard discovers Shellie is pregnant, he comes after her. Tony knows he can't keep Shellie safe on his own, considering the man's extensive network of just-as-abusive friends. Tony flees back to his brother's side.

Tony is surprised to learn Jerome is in a relationship with a guy, but that's not the biggest shock. His brother is living on a ranch . . . full of vampires. Not only that, but the second-in-command of the vampires, Kellan Harlon, expresses an interest in him. While Tony's first instinct is to run, he resists. Shellie needs him, and Kellan and his vampires can keep them safe.

Will Tony give in to Kellan's seduction before his need to bolt overrides his common sense?

Chomping on the Bullet
Copyright © 2021 Charlie Richards
ISBN: 978-1-4874-3228-7
Cover art by Angela Waters

Published by eXtasy Books Inc or
Devine Destinies, an imprint of eXtasy Books Inc

Look for us online at:
www.eXtasybooks.com or www.devinedestinies.com

Chomping on the Bullet
A Loving Nip Book Twenty-Four

By

Charlie Richards

DEDICATION

Families are like fudge – mostly sweet with a few nuts.
~Unknown

CHAPTER ONE

As Tony Harsnen rolled his overheating car to a stop in the *Burger King* parking lot, he silently cursed up a storm.

Forty-five more miles. Why couldn't the damn thing have lasted just forty-five more miles?

Tony had known that the bullets Shellie's ex-husband's friend had shot at his car when they'd been fleeing had to have hit something important.

That just seems to be her luck lately, and I've been drawn into it.

With a mental wince, Tony knew that wasn't fair. Shellie Desprow had befriended him instantly when he'd moved to Detroit for his new job. She'd shown him around the area, pointed him in the direction of the best pizza joints, and explained what areas that, as a gay man, he would be wise to avoid.

Shellie's friendship had been invaluable in helping him to settle in with a minimum of loneliness. It had been the first time he'd lived on his own, and it wasn't even in the same state, let alone city, as his brother, Jerome. His brother had taken him in when his parents had disowned him at the age of fifteen. Tony had been so worried when he'd shown up at Jerome's doorstep, but upon hearing what had happened, his brother had growled under his breath, muttered *assholes*, and made up the sofa bed.

The next day, Tony had found Jerome at the small dining room table with his laptop, looking at listings for two-bedroom apartments.

"I suppose that smoke escaping from under the hood isn't

a good thing."

Shellie's quiet comment pulled Tony out of his musings.

Reaching over, Tony placed his hand over hers and gave it a gentle squeeze. "Don't worry. We'll be okay." He pointed at the restaurant. "Let's get some food and put our heads together. We'll think of something."

"And go pee," Shellie muttered as she pushed out of the vehicle.

Tony smiled a little as he climbed from behind the wheel of his sedan. Peering over the hood of the car at Shellie, he took in her stance. She had one hand on the hood and the other on her lower back, and she was stretching a little, accentuating her rounded, pregnant stomach.

"You could have told me you needed to stop," Tony told her before reaching into the cab and pulling the hood release. "I would have stopped."

"I know you would have," Shellie replied with a grimace and a blush. "But you said your brother's place was only another forty miles, so I was trying to hold it."

Accepting that, Tony offered, "Head in, and I'll catch up. I want to check under the hood."

"Do you think you might be able to figure it out?" she asked as she began moving her six-month pregnant body in that direction.

Tony wasn't even going to pretend to know anything about cars. "Nope," he replied honestly. "But in car shows, I've always seen people popping the hood to let out the smoke and make certain nothing is burning."

Shellie nodded, then picked up her pace.

After watching Shellie disappear into the fast-food restaurant, Tony opened the hood. Gray smoke billowed up. He straightened and took a step backward, waving his hand to clear it.

Tony waited until the smoke cleared, then stared at the engine.

Yup. No inspiration striking.

With a shake of his head, Tony turned and headed into the restaurant. The restroom sounded good to him, too. As he entered, his nostrils were assailed by the scent of burgers and fries, and his stomach growled.

With his mouth watering, Tony quickly headed to the men's room and took care of business. He found Shellie standing near the line opening. She was staring at the offerings and nibbling her bottom lip.

Tony could guess exactly what she was thinking. What could they afford? They didn't have much cash left. Tony had his debit card, but he knew that the second he used it, Shellie's ex-husband would most likely be notified of where they were. Without wheels to make a quick getaway, Tony couldn't take the chance.

"There's a deal on their *Whoppers*," Tony pointed out. "Two for five bucks. And we can split a large fry."

Shellie smiled with relief. "Okay."

Tony started them toward the register. "Do you want bacon on yours?" He was pretty sure that wouldn't put them over the ten dollar bill he had in his wallet.

"Mmmm, bacon," Shellie muttered, rubbing her rounded belly.

Chuckling, Tony winked at her. "Totally."

After placing their orders, asking for cups for water, Tony put his arm around his pregnant friend and guided her toward a table. "Now we just need to find a phone."

"Too bad there are no payphones anymore," Shellie murmured, her brows creasing in concern. "We could have called collect."

As Tony nodded, Shellie's brows lifted, and a smile lit her features. "Sit and listen for the food." Grinning, she whispered, "I have an idea."

"What?" Tony asked even as he obeyed.

With a wink, Shellie bent and pressed a kiss to Tony's cheek while whispering, "Everyone likes to help pregnant ladies."

Tony wasn't too sure about that. Shellie's ex-husband, Barry Kondrin, and his friends were proof of that. Still, he wasn't going to rain on his friend's parade.

That didn't stop him from watching like a hawk as Shellie walked slowly toward a nearby table where two men sat. They both peered up at the same time, glanced at her belly, then focused on her face again.

Shellie's smile appeared hesitant as she stated, "I'm sorry to interrupt. I'm a little embarrassed really, but, um"—she pointed at the cellular phone one of them had placed on the table—"can I borrow your phone? Mine is dead, and my friend dropped his, and it broke a few days ago." Wringing her hands, Shellie peered out the window at their vehicle, which still had the hood raised. "We're having car trouble, and we need to call his brother to pick us up."

"Oh, yeah, absolutely," the dark-haired man said with a smile. "Here." He picked up the phone, woke it, and tapped on it—maybe to enter a password—before holding it out to her. "Let me know if you need any other help."

"Thank you so much," Shellie replied with a look of relief, taking the phone. "I'll get this right back to you."

After another round of *no problems* and *you're welcomes*, Shellie returned to their table. She took a seat and handed over the phone.

"That was awfully nice of him," Tony commented as he took it.

"Definitely."

Tony quickly dialed Jerome's number, glad his brother hadn't bothered to change it yet after moving to another state. Up until a few months before, he'd been in Texas, where they were both born. Then Jerome's best friend, Stanton, had fallen in love with a guy visiting from out of state, and both men had moved to Montana.

When Jerome had told Tony that he was living on a cattle ranch, he'd begun laughing . . . until his brother had assured him that he was telling the truth. He'd been shocked that his down-to-earth brother had picked up and moved without a plan in place. Jerome had even been jobless for a couple of months before finding a new one—something Tony would never have believed possible.

Except, when Tony dialed his brother's number, it rang twice before being disconnected. He frowned and dialed again, but had the same response. Growling under his breath, he muttered, "Pick up, damn it."

As if on cue, Jerome obeyed. "Whoever the fuck this is, it better be damn important," his brother snapped, sounding somewhat breathless.

"Jerome? It's Tony."

"Tony?" Jerome's voice became quieter, but Tony still heard his words. "Hang on, Cain. It's my brother." Then Jerome asked, "Is this a new number? What happened to your old phone?"

Confused, Tony wondered who Cain was, but he figured he could ask another time. When Tony and Shellie had fled her abusive ex-husband, they'd both left their phones behind. He glanced around furtively, unwilling to tell his brother everything in such a public place.

Instead, Tony lowered his voice and went with, "I'm in a bit of trouble, and I was on my way to see you, uh, to ask for some help, and my car broke down. I don't have my phone on me, so I borrowed one." Hearing his name called by someone at the counter, Tony rose from his seat, waving at Shellie to stay put. "I'm in Twin Falls, about forty miles north of you." As Tony took the tray of food, he gave the woman behind the counter a smile of thanks even as he continued, "I coasted into the *Burger King* parking lot, so we're hanging out inside."

"You're in Twin Falls?" Jerome suddenly sounded more alert. "Really?" Once again, his voice lowered. "Hand me my jeans, Cain. We gotta go."

"Of course."

That's definitely a man's voice.

"Uh, Jerome?" Tony could no longer contain his curiosity. "Who's Cain?"

"You'll meet him when we get there, and I'll explain." Jerome let out a sigh so loud it came through the line clearly. "I can hear it in your voice that something else is going on, but I'm going to wait to ask."

His brother was as intuitive as ever.

"Yeah," Tony confirmed.

"And we'll both have a bit of explaining to do." Jerome sounded uneasy as he added, "Please know I never meant to keep anything from you. I just wasn't certain how to explain . . . and it's new for me."

"Uhhhh . . . okay." Tony didn't know what else to say as he took his seat. Grabbing a French fry as he watched Shellie snag one paper-wrapped burger, he stated, "Whatever it is, we're family. We'll get through it."

Geez, I hope he feels that way when he discovers the problems I'm dragging his way.

"Absolutely," Jerome immediately replied. "Just sit tight. We'll be there soon."

"Thanks, bro."

After hanging up, Tony realized he didn't know who *we* were.

"I'll give that back to the guys," Shellie offered, perhaps sensing that Tony needed a moment to wrap his brain around his brother's cryptic words.

Tony nodded and handed it over. Popping a fry into his mouth, he chewed thoughtfully.

What was going on with his brother? He'd never mentioned any problems. Who was Cain?

Realizing he couldn't answer any of those questions right then, Tony knew he would just have to wait. He grabbed his *Whopper* and unwrapped part of it. Lifting it to his lips, he took a big bite. Tony hummed as he chewed, appreciating the flavor of the delicious burger.

He watched the man who'd lent them his phone touch the cheekbone of his eye, then point at Shellie. He said something in a soft tone while cutting a look Tony's way.

Shellie's cheeks pinked as she shook her head. "No, absolutely not," she replied, her voice carrying to Tony. "This was done by my ex-husband," she told him. "Tony is my friend, and he would never hit me."

Tony winced as he understood what the men had quietly asked about. One of the reasons they'd run was because Barry had ignored the restraining order against him. He'd shown up at Tony's place where Shellie had been staying and had smacked her around a few times before Tony had arrived home and put a stop to it. She was hiding bruises on her face underneath her concealer, but an observant eye could spot them.

Evidently, the man had noticed.

Shellie returned to her seat, a commiserating smile curving her lips. "Sorry about that," she murmured.

Shaking his head, Tony told her, "You don't need to apologize to me. It's nice to see someone concerned about the welfare of a stranger." With a wink, Tony rose from his seat. "I'm going to grab some ketchup. Want some?"

"Yes, please."

Tony squeezed Shellie's shoulder lightly as he passed, earning him a much more relaxed-looking smile from his friend.

Just over thirty minutes later, Tony noticed two cars parking beside his sedan, one on either side. The first was a large, dark-brown truck. The second appeared to be a black, high-end SUV, not that he could have said what kind.

Tony's lack of abilities with cars wasn't restricted to fixing them. Unless there were certain blatant symbols on them, he couldn't tell one brand from another.

His stomach had just begun to churn, threatening to expel his recently eaten food, when the truck's passenger door opened, and Jerome slid from the vehicle.

Relief flooding him, Tony smiled at Shellie. "That's my brother. Come on."

Tony stood, tossing all their trash onto the tray. As Shellie rose to her feet, he hurried and threw everything away. Then he met her beside the door and opened it for her.

As Tony exited the building, his gaze strayed to the men climbing out of the SUV. There were three of them, but the guy who'd been driving snagged his attention. His lean and toned frame filled out his jeans and flannel shirt in the best way possible. While Tony had never been into cowboys before, he suddenly found he might be changing his mind.

The brown-haired man in boots betrayed a confidence as he swept his gaze over the area that Tony found sexy.

Then Tony's focus was yanked away by Jerome wrapping him in a bear hug. "It's great to see you, Tony," his brother greeted jovially.

Returning his brother's embrace, Tony grinned at him. "Great to see you, too. Been too long."

Over three years since Jerome's last vacation, to be exact.

"I should have come to see you before settling here, but—" Jerome's brows furrowed as he eased his hold. The auburn-haired man standing nearby issued a soft growl, which caused Jerome to laugh and shake his head. "This is Cain Whistler. He's, well." Then Jerome cleared his throat and laid a bombshell at Tony's feet. "He's my lover."

Gaping, Tony couldn't help the shock. "Since when are you gay?"

With a smirk, Jerome countered, "Since when do you knock up chicks?"

CHAPTER TWO

K ellan Harlon glanced between Jerome and the man who was clearly his brother, Tony. While there was a definite family resemblance, there were differences, too, and it wasn't just the hair. While Jerome favored shaving his head, his couple of inches shorter brother had grown his black hair and twisted them into dozens of six-inch or so braids around his head.

I wonder what they feel like?

The desire snapped Kellan out of his stare. He blinked as he heard Jerome tease his brother about knocking up a chick, his comment easily heard with his enhanced vampire hearing, even from where he and his companions stood beside the SUV twenty feet away from the group. For some reason, he wanted to scowl at the clearly pregnant woman standing to Tony's left, wringing her hands, her stance screaming of uncertainty.

Good, she should be unsure of herself. If she lays one hand on Tony, I'm going to —

What the hell?

As the second — or second-in-command — of his vampire coven, Kellan hadn't experienced such odd reactions in centuries. He was always in control and comfortable with himself. Others thought confidence was his middle name.

When Jerome had told him that Tony was in the next town over, coming for an unexpected visit because he needed help, Kellan had rounded up Enforcers Pichette and Strauss and had told the human they were joining him. He needed to assess how difficult it would be to keep their secret. While Jerome was mated to a red fox shifter and knew about vampires, there was very little chance that Tony was also in the know about paranormals.

"I didn't knock her up," Tony replied with a roll of his eyes. He took a step back and looped his arm through hers, betraying their familiarity. "This is Shellie Desprow, my best friend. I've told you about her."

Relief flooded Kellan upon hearing those words.

Best friends. Okay.

Jerome grinned as he held out his hand. "I knew who you were, Shellie," he claimed. "I was just giving my little brother shit. I hope I didn't embarrass you."

"It's fine," Shellie replied, shaking his hand. "It's nice to finally meet you. Tony has told me so much about you." Then her brows furrowed as she glanced between Jerome and Cain. "Except that you're in a relationship."

Grimacing, Jerome nodded as he rested his hand on Tony's shoulder. "I'm sorry I didn't tell you, Tony." He glanced at Cain before refocusing on his brother. "We've only been together about a month." Scratching the back of his neck, Jerome explained, "I wanted to tell you in person, but you kept putting me off when I offered to visit."

Tony sighed as he admitted, "I didn't want you to come because I didn't want you drawn into our trouble with Shellie's ex-husband." His expression turned pained as he stared at Jerome beseechingly. "But I can't get us out of this on my own, and I didn't know who else to trust."

Kellan's gut twisted. A desire to be the one Tony trusted, the one he turned to in times of need, coiled within him. He wanted to cross the parking lot, pull the lithe black human into his arms, and soothe him, to promise he would take care of everything.

Why?

Kellan didn't know if he wanted to move closer or farther away from the human that confounded his instincts. Never one to run away from his problems, he started moseying closer to the group. He intended to catch Cain's eye so he could get an introduction.

Ten feet away from the brothers, the wind shifted. Instead of grease and food from the fast-food restaurant, Kellan smelled something else. The masculine flavor mixed with a hint of iron caused his mouth to water and his fangs to ache.

I want to taste that!

Suddenly, his odd reactions began to make sense to Kellan. Even without scenting Tony's blood, his vampiric instincts had kicked in. There was an extremely high probability that Tony was his beloved—the other half of his soul.

Only tasting the human's blood would confirm it one hundred percent.

How can I make that happen . . . as soon as possible?

Enforcer Strauss cleared his throat while smiling. "Hey, guys," he greeted. Then he glanced between them pointedly. "Maybe this isn't the best place to have this kind of conversation."

"Of course, Strauss," Cain responded instantly. With a smile, he asked, "Do you have a hotel room planned already? Or"—he paused a second, meeting Kellan's gaze—"I know there's one room at the bunkhouse available . . . and the pull-out sofa—"

Realizing Cain was floundering with how to offer them space, Kellan smiled warmly at them and held out his hand to Tony. "I'm Kellan Harlon. I co-own the ranch with a couple of friends."

On paper, that was true. He shared the ranch with coven master Dante Mannis and head enforcer Monte Hanover. Even if ranch business decisions were decided by the three of them, that didn't change the fact that Master Dante led the coven itself.

The second Tony slid his palm into Kellan's hand, the hairs on his arm stood on end. It took every bit of self-control he had to keep from tugging the human into his arms. He longed to taste his mouth, nip his bottom lip, and sip at his blood.

"N-Nice to m-meet you," Tony stuttered.

Between that and the sudden infusion of masculine arousal filling the air around him, Kellan knew he wasn't the only one being effected.

Excellent.

"The pleasure is all mine," Kellan assured, squeezing Tony's hand lightly. He didn't release right away. Instead, he rested his second hand against the human's, cradling it between both of his own. "You and your friend are welcome to join us at the ranch. I'll call ahead and have rooms prepared at the main house for you both, if it would make you more comfortable." Knowing he had to include Shellie in the offer, Kellan focused on the woman. "How far along are you, my dear? I'm sure you'd love to put your feet up for a while. We'll take you to the ranch as soon as possible."

Tony tugged a little, but Kellan refused to release him quite yet. He didn't want to lose contact. Instead, he told him, "Do you wish to get your luggage from your car? Pichette can stay with Jerome and Cain and help them tow your vehicle. The SUV will be much more comfortable for your friend."

Kellan had no qualms about using the pregnant friend to manipulate Tony a little. He wanted the man near.

"Oh, um." Tony peered Jerome's way, a question in his gorgeous brown eyes.

"I'll ride with you, too," Jerome stated, arching a brow at Kellan in silent question. As soon as Kellan nodded just a smidge, giving him silent confirmation, Jerome added, "Cain and Pichette can handle the towing, and it'll give you time to give me crap about not telling you about Cain right away." He sobered as he added, "Once we get to the ranch, we'll need you to tell me and a few others about what's going on."

Although Tony's scent soured a smidge, he still nodded. "Yeah. Okay." He once again attempted to free his hand.

Knowing he needed to release the human, and with the need to confirm that Tony was his beloved driving him, Kellan lifted the man's hand to his lips. He noted Tony's surprised scent even as he pressed a soft kiss to his flesh. Ever-so-gently, Kellan used a fang to nick Tony's flesh only to swipe his tongue over it to soothe away the sting.

Even as Kellan registered Tony's gasp of surprise, the sweet ambrosia of his blood teased his taste buds, confirming his suspicions.

My beloved. Exquisite.

Knowing the other half of his soul was standing right in front of him — *after waiting for so long, he's finally here* — Kellan barely managed to release him. Except, Jerome was now staring at him warily. His fellow paranormals, however, all wore similar looks of happiness. It didn't take much for a paranormal to realize one of their own had found their other half.

"So, your luggage?" Kellan asked, taking a small step away from Tony.

"And what the fuck happened to your car?" Jerome suddenly demanded loudly. Pointing at the grill and fender, he stated, "Those are bullet holes."

"Uhhhh . . ." Tony mumbled.

"Someone is after you, aren't they?" Enforcer Pichette stated gruffly, his hazel eyes narrowing. "That's why you both left the city without telling anyone, had to borrow a cell phone, and you're hiding bruises under make-up." Pichette pointed at Shellie.

Kellan managed to tear his gaze off his beloved long enough to really look at the woman. True enough, there was the slight discoloration of a several-day-old bruise hidden beneath the make-up along her left cheekbone. Someone had clearly hit the woman.

Asshole.

"Who?" Kellan snarled, stepping close to Tony again. Protective instincts roared through him. "Are you injured as well?"

Tony took a step backward, lifting his hands in placation — or to ward him away. "No, I'm not injured." Then he scowled. "Well, I guess I am, but it's nothing."

Kellan wanted to demand to see what Tony was talking about, but he didn't. From the uneasy scents pouring off both humans, he knew his aggression wasn't going to help matters. Instead, Kellan gave in to the need to get his beloved somewhere safe . . . like his coven territory.

"We'll discuss it all at the house," Kellan declared, resting his hand on Tony's lower back. "Let's get your stuff and get out of here."

Except, Tony just stared up at him in confusion.

Jerome stepped in, gripping his brother's upper arm and tugging him a step away from Kellan. "Do you have much shit, Tony?" he asked before turning his attention to Shellie. "Do you want to sit in the SUV? They have nice captain's chairs in the middle."

"I, um, yes, please," Shellie replied softly.

Strauss immediately stepped to her side and wrapped a thick arm around her waist. "Come on, darlin'," he drawled. "Let's get you comfortable." As the friendly and personable enforcer led Shellie away, he asked, "So, do you know if you're having a girl or a boy?"

"A boy," Shellie replied.

"Oh, yeah? Are you happy about that, or did you want a girl?" Enthusiasm filled Strauss's voice. "One of these years, I'm gonna find me a sweetheart to give me one of both." A chuckle filled his tone as he added, "Someday."

"I never really cared," Shellie replied quietly. "As long as they're healthy and nowhere near my asshole ex."

"Gotcha. Don't worry," Strauss told her confidently.

"Whoever he is, he won't touch one hair on you or your babe's head ever again."

Kellan silently seconded that vow as he turned his attention back to the others. Cain and Pichette were inspecting the bullet holes and peering under the hood. Jerome had drawn Tony toward the rear of the vehicle, and they had the back door open.

As Kellan watched Tony reach into the rear seat, he admired the way the human's jeans cradled his ass.

Gorgeous.

Then Kellan heard Tony whisper, "Is that Kellan guy always so handsy?"

Jerome responded by chuckling softly and saying, "Not in the least. He seems to be a bit taken with you. What do you think of him?" The human cut a look Kellan's way, although Tony couldn't see it because he was still pulling stuff from the car and placing it on the hood, so Kellan smiled at him. Jerome continued, "I know he's single, and everyone at the ranch says he's good to work for. You could do a lot worse."

Finally, Tony straightened and glanced Kellan's way, so Kellan pretended to be peering under the hood with the others.

"I'm bringing trouble to his ranch, Jerome," Tony whispered. "I seriously doubt he's going to have any interest in me after I explain everything."

Kellan silently vowed to prove his beloved wrong . . . and soon.

CHAPTER THREE

Sitting in a middle captain's chair with Shellie in another beside him, Tony listened as Jerome told him about how he'd met Cain. It seemed there had been some resistance on both sides at first. Jerome admitted he hadn't been certain he wanted to try a relationship with a guy, even if he made his heart race faster than anyone he'd ever met.

Tony could honestly say that he had never heard his brother say something like that before.

In the end, Jerome had approached Cain, only to find out the man was engaged . . . to a woman. His brother told him of how Cain had been planning to marry the woman because he thought he'd gotten her pregnant during a drunken one-night stand. He'd been trying to do the right thing for his unborn child.

When Cain had learned it had all been a hoax, he'd broken it off with the woman and pursued Jerome.

Hearing that Cain had lost most of his family due to his decision, Tony reached back and squeezed his brother's knee. He knew all about how that felt.

"Well, we'll just have to be all the family he needs then, huh?" Tony told Jerome. Then he leveled a fierce frown upon his brother. "As long as he treats you right."

Jerome laughed, grinning broadly. "Oh, he treats me right." Wincing, he admitted, "I'm the one more liable to screw up, since I'm still getting the hang of this relationship thing, and not just because he's a guy." Smiling crookedly at

Tony, Jerome reminded him, "Never been in one, remember?"

Tony scoffed softly. "Yeah, you were too busy caring for me, then caring for Stanton."

He knew some considered Jerome's gentle giant best friend a little slow upon first meeting, but nothing could have been further from the truth. Stanton was a creative person at heart. While a bricklayer by trade, his mosaics were always a work of art.

"So, what are you doing about your job?" Jerome asked, leaning forward with his forearms on his knees. "What'd that asshole say when you asked for time off without much notice?"

Grimacing, Tony knew Jerome was talking about Trent, his boss. The man was a total douche who would take credit for other people's work whenever he could. On the flip side, if Trent ever screwed up, he always managed to find a way to blame it on someone else.

"The asshole refused to give me time off, so I quit," Tony stated, bracing himself for the blowout.

It was immediate.

"What the hell?" Jerome barked. "Didn't you tell him it was a family emergency or something? Surely he couldn't have denied you for that."

Tony shrugged as he told his brother, "Unfortunately, there's this new girl at work who is totally sucking up to Trent. She overheard Shellie and I talking about her ex-husband troubles at lunch one day." Grimacing, he clenched his hands together in frustration, admitting, "I made a comment about coming out to the ranch to get away from him, and she told Trent about it, so when both of us wanted the time off at the same time, he refused to accept that it could be a family emergency without proof. A call from a doctor or something."

"It was getting to be a toxic environment, anyway," Shellie

murmured, reaching over and placing her hand on his arm. Peering at Jerome, she told him, "I'd already started looking for a new job, but it was hard since it's obvious I'm pregnant and will need to take maternity leave soon."

"Well, you'll have plenty of time and fresh air to relax at the ranch," Kellan stated from the front passenger seat.

Tony felt certain the lithe rancher's dark-brown eyes held a hungry gleam as he met his gaze. It caused his heartrate to speed up and his palms to sweat. Then the man blinked and turned his attention to Shellie, the look gone.

"We're happy to have you for however long you need, so try to relax," Kellan told her. "Now, you mentioned your asshole ex-husband several times. Is he the one you're running from?"

Shellie nodded. "Him and several of his friends. I left him six months ago before I knew I was pregnant." She rested her hands on her stomach, rubbing lightly. "Even if I'd known, I still would have left him. He's not a fit man to be a parent, and he always claimed he never wanted kids."

Grumbling under his breath, Tony cut in, "The only reason he's trying to take him from you is because he doesn't want to have to pay child support." Sadness filled him as he reached over and took Shellie's hand. "And to hurt you."

"I know." Shellie squeezed his hand back, clinging to him. "He's a total douchebag and a half."

Tony chuckled as he nodded. "Yeah." Frowning, he admitted, "I just have no clue how he got Pedro to take those potshots at us. He's a cop for godsake."

"A cop put those bullet holes in your car?" Strauss asked, sounding incredulous.

Tony nodded. "Barry has been having his friends follow Shellie whenever he has to work." Rolling his eyes, he added, "Unless she's at work, too." He shook his head and waved his hand absently. "Anyway, we gave Nester the slip, but he must have told Pedro. He pulled us over, said it was for speeding, and when he tried to impound my car, I took off."

"You fled a cop?" Jerome sounded shocked.

If Tony's skin hadn't been such a dark brown, he knew he would be blushing. "Yeah." Forging ahead, he added, "So he chased us." A shiver worked down his spine as he remembered Pedro's creepy smile as he'd pointed the revolver at him. "I slammed on the brakes and veered behind him, and he unloaded a couple of rounds into the car."

A shudder racked Tony's body as he recalled the harrowing experience. The tires had skidded on damp asphalt from that afternoon's rain. The creak of metal and squeal of tires had filled his ears as he'd spun around a corner too fast. His heart had been hammering a mile a minute, and fear had permeated him every time he'd checked his mirrors without seeing pursuit, which made no sense to him.

He'd always been an upstanding citizen, having never even received a parking ticket. Never would he have thought he would end up fleeing from a crooked cop.

Or maybe he's just a bullying asshole.

The feel of a strong hand squeezing his knee drew Tony's attention forward again. It also caused warmth to trickle up his leg. The hairs on his thigh lifted, sending more sensations across his skin.

"You're safe, Tony," Kellan told him, his tone serious while his brown eyes held a warmth that caused Tony's unease to melt. "We won't allow anything to happen to you." After a second, Kellan added, "Or Shellie."

Staring into Kellan's gorgeous brown eyes, Tony felt safe for the first time in weeks. He smiled at the rancher as his heartrate picked up again.

God, this guy is sexy.

"Why are you helping us?" Shellie asked softly.

Tony kind of wondered the same thing, even though he worried about what the answer would be, too.

Kellan hummed and lifted his hand, which Tony immediately missed the warmth of. The man turned his strong frame as much as possible in the seat and met Shellie's gaze squarely. "There are several reasons, my dear," Kellan told her.

The endearment, although probably only meant to reassure, sent a spike of jealousy through Tony's gut. He wanted to hear Kellan say those sorts of things directed at him. Tony also wanted Kellan's warm gaze back on him, too.

Knowing he had no cause to the feelings, he mentally tried to squash them, but damn, was it difficult. He couldn't remember the last time he'd been so instantly attracted to another man.

"First, we consider Jerome extended family, so the same would be said for Tony and by extension you." Kellan's smile appeared kind, and his tone had turned soothing. "Also, we hate bullies. No one should be forced into an uncomfortable situation just because someone else has more power." Curving his lips into a malicious-looking smirk, Kellan explained, "We love showing others that there's always a bigger fish."

"Do you do that to people who don't deserve it?" Shellie asked, cocking her head while her brows furrowed.

Kellan chuckled as he shook his head. "No, we do our best to always check facts first." Pointing out the windows, he claimed, "We may look like backwoods cowboys and ranchers, but we have state-of-the-art technology in our security center."

"Security center?" Tony asked curiously. "Why would a cattle ranch need a security center?"

Strauss barked a laugh as he glanced at them in his rearview mirror. "Cattle rustlers aren't just relegated to tales of the old west," he claimed. "We run thousands of head of cattle, and our bulls are damn expensive. We keep track of everything with cameras and electronic tags."

Nodding, Kellan explained, "Gotta know where your fifty-thousand dollar bull is at all times."

"Holy crapballs," Shellie whispered. "Fifty-thousand?"

Humming, Kellan winked at her. "Yes, ma'am."

"So, you guys spend your free time helping people in trouble?" Tony asked slowly, processing that. "Like *The Equalizer* or something?"

Glancing over his shoulder, revealing that he was grinning, Strauss commented, "That actually sounds like it would be a lot of fun. I love those movies."

As Strauss turned back around, Tony thought he spotted an odd sharpness to the man's canines. He was about to dismiss it when he realized he didn't have much of an imagination. He also recalled the soft nip Kellan had placed on the back of his hand. At the time, Tony had been too shocked to make much of it.

Does Kellan have pointy teeth like that, too? If so, what would be their purpose?

"We're here," Jerome murmured into Tony's ear, making him jolt.

"What?" Tony peered around, realizing the vehicle had stopped, Shellie had already exited, and only Jerome remained inside with him, and he'd moved to take over Shellie's seat beside him. If Tony had to guess, he figured the others were giving him and his brother a few minutes alone. "Damn, I zoned, didn't I?"

Jerome nodded. "Not surprising, really." He rested his hand on his shoulder and squeezed. "It sounds like you've been going through a lot. How come you didn't tell me sooner?"

Knowing it was time to come clean, Tony admitted, "I wanted to do it on my own."

Cocking his head, Jerome asked, "Why?" When Tony hesitated, Jerome added, "I'm your brother. I'll always be there for you. No matter what."

Tony smiled and nodded. "I know. Believe me, I know." Unbuckling his seatbelt, he turned in his seat to face his brother fully. "I could always count on you, but I've been standing on my own feet for so long . . . and I never wanted to go back to the scared boy who was afraid his brother would turn his back on him, too."

Jerome shook his head, his smile appearing kind. Understanding gleamed in his big brother's eyes. "You've come a long way from the stuttering mess our parents turned their back on." Taking Tony's hands between his own, he added, "Just the way you're trying to take care of your best friend who is carrying the baby of an asshole tells me exactly the kind of amazing man you've grown up to be, and I couldn't be prouder."

"Thank you," Tony whispered, blinking quickly to clear the unexpected sheen from his eyes. "That's why I bit the bullet and tried to come to you."

"I'm glad, and with that said," Jerome continued, his tone turning serious. "Not sharing your troubles with me makes me want to smack you upside the head." His smile turned wry as his eyes twinkled. "Now, if you'd told me a couple of months ago about the problems you and Shellie were facing, I don't know if I could have done much but give you a safe place to move to far away from the bastard." Jerome sobered as he peered out the window toward a massive ranch house. "These guys, though . . . these guys will be able to help with shit like that."

"Really?" Tony felt a fresh shiver of unease. "They aren't engaged in something illegal or anything, right?"

Jerome laughed as he shook his head. "No. Definitely nothing illegal." With a wink, he released Tony and began sliding from the vehicle. "Cain is a deputy. Didn't I tell you that?"

"No, you didn't," Tony replied, following him from the SUV, then falling into step with him. "So . . . what's up with these guys?"

Grinning, Jerome clapped his hand on the back of Tony's neck and squeezed affectionately. "From the way Kellan was looking at you, I'm damn sure you'll know everything very shortly."

Tony wanted to ask more, but then they were climbing the porch steps, and someone was opening the front door for them. Their brotherly alone time was at an end.

CHAPTER FOUR

"Y ou're certain?"

Upon hearing Master Dante's question, Kellan turned from the window. As soon as he'd entered, he'd located the vampire master as well as Monte. All three were in the upstairs library rather than the study because it faced the front of the house.

That had afforded Kellan with a view of the SUV where Jerome had stayed behind to speak with Tony. At some point on the way home, his human had zoned out. Jerome had whispered that it happened sometimes when Tony was mentally overwhelmed and needed to process, and Shellie must have overheard because she'd nodded as she cast a worried look Tony's way.

Then Jerome had encouraged everyone to head into the house.

That hadn't stopped Kellan from finding the window with the best view of the SUV. That had been the library.

"Kellan?"

Realizing he'd ignored Master Dante's question in favor of returning his attention to the window, Kellan turned enough to see both his master and the SUV. He grinned widely as he nodded. "Yes, Dante. I'm certain. I tasted his blood."

"In front of his brother?" Monte smirked at him, his green eyes twinkling. "That must have been awkward."

As Dante chuckled, Kellan realized to what Monte was referring. The saliva of a vampire mixed with their bite, creating so much pleasure that a donor would orgasm. On the flip side, if a vampire refused to mix saliva into the wound, their bite would be damn near excruciating.

Kellan had never seen any reason to do that to a human, and to his knowledge, neither had his friends.

Shaking his head, Kellan scowled at Monte. "Of course, I wouldn't do that to my beloved. I nicked him on his hand while kissing it just enough to taste his blood." Taking the tumbler of whiskey from Dante, Kellan murmured his thanks before adding, "Best I can tell is it probably tingled and caused his blood to warm with a bit of extra arousal."

"Well, congratulations," Dante stated before taking a sip of his drink.

"Thank you." Kellan couldn't help but grin. "It's about damn time."

"Indeed it is," Monte agreed. Crossing to the window, he sipped his own drink. "So, when are you going to ease him into our world?"

Kellan knew the enforcer referred to the knowledge that paranormals existed and vampires specifically. *Well, shifters, too, I guess.* After all, Jerome was mated to a red fox shifter.

With that thought in mind, Kellan stated, "I know Jerome will help. He understands the pull."

"Jerome is a good man," Dante stated. "Of course, he'll help. Stanton, too." Cocking his head, he narrowed his eyes. "Ah, they're exiting the vehicle. Time to find out everything about their problems."

More than on board with that, Kellan turned away from the window, eager to be in his beloved's presence once more. Judging by the soft thud of boots following him, he knew Dante and Monte followed. He was halfway down the stairs that overlooked the foyer when Strauss opened the front door, allowing him to view his handsome beloved again.

Kellan's mouth watered with his desire to taste Tony's full lips. He wanted to skim his hands over his beloved's dark skin so badly that his fingers almost twitched hard enough to cause him to fumble his tumbler of whiskey. With the way his blood flowed into his prick, Kellan hoped he wasn't sporting a blatantly raging boner.

I can't remember the last time I lost control of my body like this.

Considering his beloved was staring up at his approaching form with a hint of hunger in his dark eyes, Kellan didn't mind one damn bit.

"Hello, Tony. I'm Dante Mannis," the master began, reaching the bottom of the stairs. He held out his hand as he continued, "The redhead is Monte Hanover. Welcome to our home."

"Uh, thank you so much for having me," Tony replied, taking Dante's hand. "I really do appreciate it."

"Any family of Jerome's and all that," Dante replied blithely, releasing the handshake. With his hand palm up, he indicated the hallway that led to the back of the house. "My wife, Ruth, is getting Shellie settled in the family room. Francois probably already has refreshments to be served. Let's go get comfortable while we discuss what brought you both here." With a knowing look, Dante added, "And I don't mean a broken-down car."

Tony nodded as he allowed Jerome to steer him through the house. "Of course, sir." He glanced at Kellan while nibbling his bottom lip, then looked at Dante again. "And if after you hear what we have to say you want us to leave, we'll both understand."

Monte snorted, the sound low and rough. "That won't happen, man." The enforcer slipped past everyone to open a set of double doors. "Make yourself comfortable, Tony."

Kellan followed as everyone trooped into the huge family room. The space was decked out with several sofas, recliners, and other choices of seating. While there was a massive television hung at one end of the room, it was currently off. Shellie was already relaxing on a reclining chair with her feet up, and Ruth had perched herself on a nearby love seat and was speaking softly with her.

When Shellie looked up and spotted Tony, her smile held a wealth of relief. "Hey, Tony. You feeling okay?"

Tony scoffed as he crossed to her. "I should be asking you that." He settled on the recliner closest to her, resting on the edge of the seat. "I'm fine. What about you?" He glanced between Ruth and Shellie. "Is everything all right?"

"I'm fine." Shellie waved away Tony's concern. "Recline in that thing. These are amazing." Then she wiggled a little in her seat and sighed. "So nice after nine hours in the car."

Chuckling, Tony nodded. "I'm sure you're right."

Before Tony could settle, the doors opened again, and Francois appeared, pushing a trolley before him. Behind him was his beloved, Stanton. The huge human grinned broadly as he lumbered into the room.

"Hey, Tony!" Stanton greeted as he crossed the room. "Great to see ya."

Tony bounced from his chair and met Stanton in the middle of the floor. The pair shared a hug full of backslaps. When Tony moaned and grabbed his back, tension flooded Kellan, and he took a step toward the pair.

Stanton laughed and rolled his eyes. "You big faker. I didn't squeeze ya that hard."

Laughing, Tony grinned. "Had ya goin' for a second there, big guy." He looked him up and down. "What the hell have these guys been feeding you? You look even more muscled than before."

Shrugging his massive boulders for shoulders, Stanton replied, "It's been four years since I seen ya last." He lifted his arms and showed off his massive biceps, the sleeves of his t-shirt straining. "Years of bricklayin' will do that to a man."

"That it will, big guy," Tony replied, grinning. "You look great."

"Thanks. You look good, too." Stanton reached up and pinched a braid between his thumb and forefinger. "When'd you do this?"

"About two years ago," Tony replied, also touching one of his braids. "I like it."

"Me, too." Stanton released the braid and rubbed his palm over his closely shorn scalp, which nearly hid the fact that his hair was dirty-blond. "Bet it's just as easy as mine."

Tony laughed, slapping Stanton on his massive bicep. "Yup. Easy is good when you suck at getting up on time in the morning."

Grinning, Stanton started leading the way toward Francois and the trays he was setting out on the sideboards. "Definitely. And when you're just too lazy or apa . . . apa . . ." His brows furrowed. "What's that word, babe?"

Francois turned, having just completed his task. "Do you mean apathetic, my beloved?" When Stanton still looked uncertain, the French vampire slipped his fingers into the crook of Stanton's elbow. "Zat means you just don't care enough to worry about it."

"Yeah!" Stanton grinned broadly. "That's the one." He pulled his arm away only to wrap it around Francois's waist and pull him close. "This is Francois. He's my partner. At the first of the year, we started this word of the day calendar where we learn a new word every day. It's cool."

Smiling at Francois, Tony nodded his head. "Great to meet you, Francois." He glanced Jerome's way before saying, "My brother has mentioned you a few times." Pointing at Stanton, Tony claimed, "You got a good one here. Treat him right."

Humming while narrowing his eyes, Francois assured, "Oh, don't you worry, Tony. Zat is somezing I will take great pleazure in doing."

Tony laughed as Stanton's cheeks took on a hint of pink.

Francois didn't draw the moment out. Instead, he pointed

at the food. "If you are hungry, help yourself." Then he pointed at the several plastic decanters he'd placed on the sideboard. "Hot drinks. Tea on zee left, coffee on zee right." Lowering his index finger, Francois finished, "And zee mini-fridge holds many ozer options."

"Wow, okay. Thanks."

Tony panned his gaze over everything. He even licked his lips, but he didn't reach for a plate or the fridge.

Kellan spotted the mixture of longing and indecision in Tony's eyes. Giving in to his instinct to help his beloved, he sidled up next to him. He grabbed a plate for them both, holding one out to Tony.

"Here, Tony," Kellan encouraged. "I know you were just at *Burger King*, but did you get enough to eat?"

"Um, no," Tony admitted, hesitantly taking the plate. "Not really."

"Well, there's plenty here." Kellan grabbed another plate and set both on the sideboard. "The one on the right is for Shellie," he told Tony, answering his silent questioning look. "What does she like?"

As Kellan waited for Tony to make up his mind, he added food to his own plate. He used a large spoon to scoop a number of crisp potato wedges onto his plate. When he filled it again, he held it over Shellie's plate. "Yes? No?"

Tony nodded. "Yes."

Kellan dumped it onto the plate, then filled the large spoon again. That time, he hovered it over Tony's plate. After seeing Tony nod, Kellan emptied the scoop.

To Kellan's relief, that was all the prompting Tony needed. He began adding items to his plate as he pointed out things for Shellie. Tony even added some things to Shellie's plate himself.

Once their plates were full, Kellan asked, "What would you both like to drink. Probably not something caffeinated for

Shellie." He'd heard that human women tended to avoid it while pregnant.

"You're right. Do you know what kind of tea Francois brought?"

Kellan would have asked Francois, but the chef and Stanton had moved away and were talking quietly with Jerome.

That's probably about me and Tony and how to deal with revealing paranormals to him.

Kellan could only hope for the support.

"Not sure." Kellan grabbed the carafe and a mug, then poured a little into it. He swigged it back and grimaced. "Ugh, Earl Grey. Probably caffeinated."

Tony chuckled. "Not a fan?"

Shaking his head, Kellan admitted, "If there's no coffee, it'll do in a pinch, but it's definitely not a preference." Then he opened the small fridge and peered at the contents. "How about juice or lemonade?" he offered as he grabbed a bottle of beer for himself. "And what about you?"

"A beer would be great," Tony conceded, so Kellan grabbed another. "And Shellie would love that pink lemonade."

Kellan had planned to tuck the beverages under his arms, but Tony had already picked up his and Shellie's plates. After threading the bottlenecks between his fingers and carrying them with one hand, he tucked three napkin-wrapped silverwares into his back pocket. Finally, Kellan grabbed his own plate and quickly followed after Tony.

Reaching the pair as Tony gave Shellie her plate, Kellan placed her bottle of lemonade on a nearby side table. Then he did the same with one of the silverware sets. When Kellan noticed Tony move toward the recliner he'd been sitting on briefly, he rested his hand on his back and urged him toward the small sofa Ruth had vacated.

To Kellan's delight, Tony obeyed.

CHAPTER FIVE

Tony and Shellie had done it. Between the two of them, they'd shared everything that had been going on for the last, well, year. On more than one occasion, Tony had wished Shellie had told him about Barry's abuse long before he'd wheedled it out of her one Saturday night.

Of course, getting drunk and pestering her about bruises that were clearly finger-holds on her arm was probably the only reason she'd finally come clean.

After that, Shellie had admitted to being done. She'd secretly met with an attorney. The man had advised her to begin documenting the abuse.

Tony had nearly gone ballistic after reading just a few pages of Shellie's notes. Only by reminding himself of how he never wanted to give his parents cause to say, I told you so, about him had stayed his hand. The pair had spouted all kinds of shit when they'd kicked him out, including plenty of comments about how gays were ruining society.

He'd figured murder would definitely make them feel justified.

Instead, Tony had helped Shellie secretly pack up her stuff and move it into his spare room. Barry had long since stopped paying attention to her unless he wanted a punching bag. He hadn't even hesitated to sign the divorce papers.

For three blissful months, they'd both thought Barry was out of their lives.

"So how the hell did Barry find out Shellie's pregnant?" Tony mused.

"What do you mean, Tony?"

Snapping his head up upon hearing Kellan's softly spoken question, Tony remembered he wasn't alone . . . like, at all. Everyone was still in the room, discussing various strategies. He and Shellie had given Monte every name they could think of that was associated with Barry. Considering Shellie had been married to the douchebag for six years, the list had been considerable.

Tony still sat beside Kellan on the small sofa. For some reason, he felt as if he'd drawn strength from the handsome rancher. The man had been attentive and thoughtful, getting him more beer, getting him ketchup for the potato wedges, and even finding him some blue cheese dressing to dip his hot wings in since all they'd had out was ranch.

Really? With the amount of wings that had been in the huge bowl, there should have been a vat of the stuff.

In Tony's opinion, ranch was a poor substitute for blue cheese on hot wings.

"Um." Tony tried to marshal his thoughts after so much food and beer. "Barry came after Shellie about his kid three months ago, but she wasn't showing at that time." He peered at his friend, trying to puzzle it out. "How the hell did he know you were pregnant?"

"I—" Shellie frowned. "You know, I have no idea." Cocking her head, she stared into the cup of chamomile tea Francois had so kindly fetched for her. "I never questioned it before. I just assumed he saw me leaving the doctors and somehow pretended to still be my husband and convinced someone there to talk to him."

"Well, let's see if we can't answer that question along with a few others," Dante stated with a cool smile. "I can't wait to see what we can find on that Pedro cop. He definitely needs to be removed from authority."

Tony silently agreed.

Monte rose, his electronic notepad in hand. "I'm going to

take this to Serval. He's already texted me twice, wanting to get more information so he can dig deeper." Scoffing, he started toward the door while adding, "Your bank accounts had been frozen and your cards monitored, and he's back-hacking to find out where those orders came from."

"What?" Tony leaned forward, suddenly feeling wide awake. "I can't even access my checking account?"

"Relax," Kellan murmured, sliding his arm around his waist. "You'll want for nothing here, giving us plenty of time to sort out this mess."

Pausing at the door, Monte stared at him with furrowed brows. "Damn, I'm sorry, man. I thought you knew." He glanced between Tony and Shellie, who nibbled her bottom lip while her eyes were wide. Her knuckles were nearly white with the firm grip she had on her cup. "I thought that was why you were sticking to cash."

Tony recalled mentioning that they'd used their cash to get to Jerome. Plus, they'd left behind their cellphones, so he figured it was an honest mistake to make.

Meeting the big man's gaze, Tony shook his head. "No." He winced as he admitted, "I was just going off of what I'd seen on television."

"Brilliant," Kellan murmured.

Then, to Tony's shock, the man leaned over and pressed a kiss to his temple. He turned to peer at the man, gaping at him.

"Tempting, tempting," Kellan murmured, using a crooked finger under Tony's chin to urge him to close his mouth. "But I'll taste your mouth another time." Lowering his voice to an intimate, husky rumbly sound that set Tony's blood on fire, Kellan purred, "After you've had a good night's sleep and you're not a little tipsy from beer and whiskey."

"It was only two shots," Tony countered with a flick of his gaze to Kellan's mouth.

Groaning, Kellan shook his head. "But you're a light-weight." Lowering his head, he kissed Tony's cheek that time. "Have patience, handsome. We have plenty of time."

Then Kellan straightened and turned his attention to Jerome.

As if on cue, Jerome rose to his feet, as did Cain, Stanton, and Francois.

"Come on, bro," Jerome urged, beckoning. He held out his hand to Shellie. "You, too, sweetheart. You've had a long couple of days. I bet you could use an early night."

"Yes, please," Shellie immediately replied, taking Jerome's hand and rising to her feet. "Some shuteye sounds delightful."

Kellan helped Tony to his feet, and when he swayed a little, he helped steady him.

"Okay. Bed is probably a good thing," Tony muttered. The stress had to be getting to him because he hadn't thought he'd drank all that much.

"Come on, little buddy." Stanton wrapped his arm around Tony's waist and began herding him toward the exit where Shellie and his brother had just disappeared through. "These guys spare no expense. Their mattresses are epic."

"Okay," Tony murmured. He peered over his shoulder, seeing Kellan watching him.

Kellan smiled. "I'll see you in the morning, handsome."

"Huh," Tony mumbled as he again faced forward. "He called me handsome."

"Yup," Stanton confirmed. "He sure did."

"He's hot." Tony realized he'd said that out loud. "Damn. What did I drink?"

"I think the stress is catching up with you," Monte told him as they passed him in the hallway. "Get some rest."

"Okay." Nodding, Tony figured that had to be right.

As Stanton helped him up the stairs, Tony noted the way a

lithe brunette woman sniffed before her eyes widened. Her focus snapped from him, then to the stairs. Following her gaze, Tony spotted Shellie disappearing to the right.

When Tony turned back to ask the woman what was wrong, she'd already fled in the direction of the family room.

Weird.

Tony woke in a bed that made him feel like he was floating on a cloud.

Amazing. I totally want one of these.

After peeling his eyes open, Tony peered slowly around the room. He didn't recognize it. Tony allowed his eyelids to slide closed again, willing his brain to wake up, too.

To Tony's relief, the events of the prior day filtered through his brain.

Driving back roads all night. Fighting the rain in the morning. Getting stranded at the restaurant.

Then my brother, his boyfriend, and his friends. Just damn.

Considering everything that had happened to him in the last twenty-four hours, Tony wasn't at all surprised that his body and mind had given out. He and Shellie had talked about stopping and sleeping in the car, but he'd been too afraid Barry and Pedro would manage to catch up to them. Instead, he'd drank nasty black coffee from gas stations and pushed through, even too afraid to allow Shellie to drive. He didn't want to put even more stress on her pregnancy.

Instead, his friend had dozed nearly all evening.

Except, Tony was safe — for the moment. He prayed that coming there wouldn't endanger his new friends. If any cops showed up looking for him, he figured he would know sooner rather than later, since Jerome's man Cain was a deputy in town.

God, and isn't that a mind trip?

As Tony pushed aside the comforter and swung his legs over the mattress, a bubble of laughter erupted from him.

"My brother is in a gay relationship."

Tony would never label another man, even his brother. He knew that Jerome had never considered himself gay, and he'd even gone to some gay clubs with Tony to gauge the atmosphere and make certain it was safe for him. His brother had definitely always leaned more toward the ladies.

That meant Cain had to be damn special to draw his brother's eye. Tony really hoped it worked out for him. His brother deserved to be happy.

With that thought in mind, Tony's mind drifted to Kellan. The man had made a blatant pass at him before he'd sent him to bed. Tony wondered if he would see any of the rancher that day.

Tony figured running a ranch, even sharing responsibilities with others, would keep him busy.

"Time for a shower, Tony," he grumbled to himself, shaking his head. Then he frowned as he turned in a circle in the middle of the room. "Aaaaand where would the bathroom even be?"

Feeling a twinge in his bladder, Tony headed toward the closest door. That one led to a closet. The second one he tried opened to a hallway. Tony tried door number three.

With a sigh of relief, Tony hustled to the toilet and emptied his bladder. After shaking off and washing his hands, he checked the drawers. He found a brand new toothbrush, which he used. Then Tony helped himself to a shower.

The hot water cascading over Tony's skin woke him up the rest of the way. He reveled in the wonderful spray, impressed with the pressure available at a place so far out in the country. Once he'd washed and dried, he wrapped the towel around his waist and returned to the main room.

That was when he spotted his backpack.

Tony scoffed as he crossed to it, knowing he must have been only half awake to have walked right past it.

Ten minutes later, Tony opened the door to the hallway again. He looked left and right, wondering which way was the correct one. Just as he began to turn left, he heard someone calling his name.

Turning, Tony found Jerome headed his way, a big grin on his face. "Hey, Sleeping Beauty. I wondered when you'd get out of bed." He beckoned. "This way to coffee."

"Oh, thank god," Tony replied on a moan, hurrying toward his brother.

Jerome laughed, slapping him on the back. "Come on."

"Is it late?" Tony asked. Without his phone, he didn't know, and he hadn't noticed a clock in his room.

Jerome shook his head. "Naw. Only almost eight-fifteen." He turned a corner, and the stairs to the large front foyer appeared. "I figured now would be about when you woke up after your crash yesterday."

"Crash?" Tony tensed. He didn't remember wrecking his car.

Nodding, Jerome glanced over his shoulder as he trotted down the stairs. "Yeah. Your system crash." His expression sobered. "I mean when your body accepted you were in a safe place and shut down on you, making you sleep for twelve hours."

Following Jerome, Tony gaped. "I slept for almost twelve hours?" He couldn't remember the last time he'd done that — probably when he'd pulled all-nighters studying for exams.

Jerome nodded. "Yup. So, do you remember everything from yesterday?"

Tony nodded back. "I do."

"Good, because Serval worked half the night, and I hear he wants to meet with the inner circle and us as soon as possible."

Confused by Jerome's words, Tony repeated, "Inner circle?"

Except, then his brother opened a doorway, revealing a dining room. The rich aroma of good coffee flooded his senses. After inhaling deeply, he groaned softly, causing Jerome to laugh.

His brother slapped him on the shoulder, saying, "Come on, Tony. Let's get you some coffee before the drool drips down your chin."

"Yes, please," he replied, too interested in a morning cup of joe to tease the man back.

CHAPTER SIX

Kellan sat at the table with Shellie and Karina—a female vampire guard and wrangler. It always amazed him how Fate could work in such mysterious ways. Not only was Tony Kellan's beloved, but Shellie was the beloved of Karina.

The woman had scented her in the foyer when Shellie had been heading up to bed the prior evening. Karina had immediately rushed to the family room to talk to Master Dante about the strangers in their midst. Unfortunately, she'd had to wait to meet her until breakfast.

I bet that was a long night for her, wondering if her instincts that the pregnant human in our midst was really her beloved.

Kellan had some idea of how Karina would have felt, too. Having his beloved under his roof but being unable to hold him had been excruciating. He'd gotten little sleep, constantly listening just in case his human needed him in the night. A couple of times, Kellan had even gotten up and lurked outside Tony's bedroom, just to hear his deep, even breathing.

While Kellan had always been an early riser—it was sort of required when working with animals—he didn't normally wander into the dining room before dawn. He'd received a knowing look from Francois as well as a steaming cup of coffee. Sitting there, he'd drank two before Shellie came in.

Karina must have been watching, for she'd appeared seconds later. After introducing herself, she'd welcomed Shellie to the ranch. Then she'd helped her with food and drink while doing her best not to appear overbearing.

Kellan was in the process of fighting the same instincts to

barrel into his beloved's life and take care of everything.

At least both of them can be told at the same time. Between Jerome and Stanton and going through the learning process together, hopefully it won't be too stressful for either of them.

"Oh, here's Tony."

Shellie's words cut into Kellan's thoughts. He saw her furrowed brows as she continued.

"I'm not surprised he slept so long. He wouldn't let me do any of the driving, staying up all night to get us here."

Kellan found Tony allowing Jerome to guide him to the coffee station. The human's focus seemed riveted on the different carafes, each labeled with what was inside. He watched carefully as his beloved chose a dark French roast, adding a small dollop of heavy cream.

Then Tony brought the mug to his nose and inhaled deeply. The look on his human's face could only be called one of bliss. Finally, still smiling, Tony sipped tentatively.

When Kellan's gut twinged, he realized he was getting jealous of a damn cup of coffee. He turned his focus to his own mug, finding it nearly empty. Taking the opportunity, he rose as he swigged back the contents, finishing it in one gulp.

Making his way to get more, Kellan admired the way Tony's worn jeans molded to his ass and legs. His polo shirt accentuated his lean torso and the strong lines of his back. Even holding the mug of coffee to his lips showcased the light muscle definition of his arms.

As Kellan drew close, Tony's masculine fragrance—mixed with a sage scent, probably soap from his shower—teased his nostrils. Between his beloved's delectable aroma and his casual masculinity, Kellan felt his body reacting. He couldn't help the way his blood flowed south, filling his prick as anticipation flooded him.

This human is mine.

Knowing he still had to undertake the task of convincing Tony, Kellan resisted the urge to sweep him into his arms and taste him.

"Good morning, Tony," Kellan greeted softly, not wanting to startle him as he continued to lean against the counter and drink his coffee. "Did you sleep well?"

Nodding, Tony hummed. He smiled at Kellan over the rim of his mug even as he continued to sip from it.

Kellan wondered at that response.

Is my beloved still tired?

"Can I get you something to eat?" Kellan asked, trying to engage him again. "What do you normally enjoy for breakfast?"

He waved his hand toward the bar holding several trays of steaming food. There was sausages, bacon, eggs with and without cheese, a couple different styles of potatoes, as well as different styles of toasted bread, including biscuits and gravy. As paranormals, vampires could easily eat more than humans, and they worked with cattle, which burned plenty of calories.

When Tony just stared at the food somewhat vacantly, Kellan tried, "I know most of that is pretty heavy. Standard fair for ranch workers." Touching Tony's elbow lightly, he told him, "There's fruit and yogurt and some lighter stuff in the fridge, if you'd prefer, and if there's something you want that isn't there, I'm certain Francois can make it."

"Ummm." Tony blinked a few times before saying, "It all looks so good."

"Hey, Shell," Jerome called to where the woman sat nearby. "I see my brother is still pretty comatose until after that first cup of coffee."

Shellie laughed as she grinned at them. "Try two, Jer."

Jerome shook his head, still smiling as he warned, "Don't try to get too much conversation out of Tony until he's had some caffeine in the morning. He's never been a morning person."

Kellan hummed, understanding. At least his human wasn't

purposefully ignoring him. He was just always like this.

"In that case, come sit and enjoy your coffee," Kellan urged. Taking Tony's arm, he guided him toward the table, saying, "We'll allow the conversation to ebb and flow around us as you wake up fully."

"'M-kay."

Chuckling softly, Kellan realized he found his beloved's spaciness adorable. He knew from watching other relationships that actually admitting that to his man wouldn't be appreciated. Instead, he sat down next to Tony and relaxed with his arm around the back of his chair. Then he took advantage of that same spaciness to tease at a couple of the short braids at the back of his head.

Kellan found the texture an odd mixture of rough and smooth, and he wondered what it would feel like sliding against his skin. Lifting his mug to his lips, he discovered it empty and chuckled. He'd been so caught up in trying to engage his beloved that he'd completely forgotten to refill his mug.

Returning to his feet, Kellan headed back to the coffee stand. He poured himself a mugful, then grabbed an empty one. Recalling Tony's preference, he made a second cup for his beloved before heading back to the table.

When Kellan placed the mug before Tony, his beloved tipped his head back to stare at him in surprise. "Thank you," he murmured, sounding grateful.

Kellan smiled down at him. "You're welcome."

Unable to resist any longer, Kellan lowered his head and pressed a soft kiss to Tony's full lips. Even though Tony gasped in surprise, he resisted deepening the kiss. Instead, Kellan swiped his tongue along his lower lip, tasting the addicting flavor of coffee and his human, before pressing a few more sipping kisses to his beloved's flesh and ending it.

Lifting his head, Kellan smiled upon spotting Tony's dazed

expression. He knew it was for a whole different reason than not being totally awake. Kellan liked it even better when Tony lifted his free hand to touch his lips.

"Wow," Tony murmured. Furrowing his brows, he asked, "What was that for?"

Unable to help himself, Kellan grinned widely. His beloved was just too damn cute.

To Kellan's dismay, Tony's brows furrowed, and his expression clouded. When his human reached up and touched his fang, he realized his mistake. Even as Tony gasped and jerked his hand back, Kellan moaned softly.

That innocent, gentle touch to his sharp canine had felt so much like a caress to his cock, and his gut clenched with a burning need as arousal rushed through him.

"Why don't you sit down, Kellan."

Kellan had no idea when Master Dante had entered the room, but he instinctively obeyed his coven leader. Sitting in the chair he'd vacated earlier, he moved to return his arm to the back of Tony's chair. Except, Tony leaned away from him, staring at him with wide eyes and parted lips.

Sighing deeply, Kellan felt as if a stake had been driven through his heart. He scented fear from his human. The tension in the man's body told him Tony fought a desire to jump up and run.

"Tony," Jerome called softly from his brother's other side. "Relax, man. You're okay." When Jerome rested his hand on Tony's shoulder, Kellan's beloved jolted in his seat. "Hey, bro. Take a deep breath. I promise everything is okay."

After a furtive glance around, Tony leaned toward Jerome and hiss-whispered, "But . . . did you see their fangs, Jer?" He glanced around again, obviously not knowing that almost all of them could hear his words. "They can't really be vampires, right? They don't exist."

Kellan guessed he was looking for reassurance that his

crazy idea was just that . . . crazy. He knew Jerome wouldn't be able to reassure him. After all, Tony's brother knew them for what they were.

"Uh, actually, they do," Jerome began slowly. "But try to relax, huh?" He rubbed his hand up and down Tony's back. "They would never hurt you."

"What the hell are you saying?" Despite Jerome's grip on his shoulder, Tony still managed to jump to his feet. "Why would you bring me here if you knew they were vampires?" Gasping, Tony asked, "Is Cain a vampire, too? Are you under his thrall?"

Jerome slowly rose to his feet while lifting both hands in placation. "Tony, I have no idea what being in a vampire's thrall is even supposed to mean." He held his brother's gaze steadily as he added, "And, no, Cain is not a vampire, and I brought you here because it's safe here, and you both needed a safe place." Jerome glanced at Kellan, his gaze questioning. "And for other reasons."

Kellan knew what Jerome was asking him. Should he tell Tony about beloveds?

Before Kellan could decide, Master Dante stepped forward. "Tony, please relax. We have much to discuss, but your safety is not one of them." Resting his hands on the back of a chair, he leaned forward a little. "You are completely safe. You're under my protection, *our* protection. Every vampire here would give their lives to save yours." Dante smiled at Shellie, who still sat at the table and stared wide-eyed, her features pale even as Karina held her hand. "You, too, Shellie. You're completely safe, and we will stop Barry."

Dante speaking Shellie's ex-husband's name seemed to penetrate Tony's rising haze of panic. "Wh-Why would you help us if you're vampires?"

Unable to remain an impassive observer with his beloved panicking, Kellan slowly rose to his feet. "We explained that to you already," he began, not liking the way Tony eased a step away from him. "You're Jerome's brother. Family." Kellan offered a faint smile in Shellie's direction before refocusing on Tony. "You both are."

"I-I'm so confused," Tony whispered.

Then his eyes rolled to the back of his head, and he began to drop.

Kellan swept Tony into his arms and cradled his human to his chest. Glancing around helplessly, he wondered what the hell he should do next. He focused on Jerome, opened his mouth, then closed it again.

"I don't remember you acting zat way when you found out about us," Francois stated, announcing his presence. A clearly concerned Stanton stood by his vampire's side as Francois continued, "Is zere somezing we should know about your brozer, Jerome?"

Jerome frowned even as he shook his head, clearly at a loss to explain Tony's behavior.

It was Shellie who shed some light on the subject. "Barry is a cheetah shifter."

"Really?" Dante asked. "And Tony knows about them?"

Shellie shook her head. "Not really. Barry started losing control of his temper when Tony was at our house once, and his canines started to grow." She nibbled her bottom lip for a second as she peered around at them all. "A few days later, I tried to figure out how much he'd noticed, but Tony had already dismissed it as my husband having a broken tooth and needing dental work." Shrugging, Shellie admitted, "I figured it would be best to just leave it at that."

"Well, it does explain some of the shit I found on Barry and Pedro," Serval stated, striding into the room. He glanced at Kellan holding Tony before moving toward the coffee station. "There's a loosely affiliated cheetah tribe in that area, and both men are part of it." With his fresh cup of coffee in hand,

Serval leaned his butt against the counter and focused on Shellie. "Your son will be a shifter cub, and that's why he wants him."

Gaping, Shellie paled. "What?"

Chapter Seven

Tony groaned softly as he slowly swam to wakefulness. His head pounded, and he felt as if he'd been hit by a semi. He'd been in a car accident once—been rear-ended on an icy road—and he hadn't felt as bad then as he did right then.

"Drink some water, Tony."

Recognizing Stanton's voice and feeling something tap against his bottom lip, Tony opened. He recognized a straw and sucked. The cool water hit his tongue, and he swallowed, relieved to feel it soothe his parched throat.

After several swallows, Stanton pulled the straw away. "How are you feeling?"

Licking his lips and swallowing a couple of more times, Tony tried to figure out the answer to that question. "What happened?" he asked instead.

"You fainted." That was Jerome's voice. "I'm going to wipe your eyes. Just stay still."

Tony nodded once, feeling embarrassed as hell.

Why did I faint?

The sensation of a damp cloth rubbing over his skin helped ease the pounding in his brain. He sighed, relaxing on the comfortable mattress.

Mattress. Comfortable. Ranch bedroom.

Vampires!

Gasping, Tony snapped his eyes open. He quickly peered around the room, taking in the occupants. When he saw only Stanton, Jerome, and Shellie, he relaxed back onto the mattress.

"Aaaand, you just remembered the conversation," Jerome commented dryly. His dark eyes held a wealth of concern as he added, "It's time to come to grips with this, Tony. The men and women here are trying to help you not hurt you."

"They're not like Barry and his friends," Shellie murmured, leaning forward in her chair. She cradled a cup of something between her palms as she eyed him pensively. "I promise."

Tony gaped at Shellie for an instant before his brain processed what she was claiming. "You knew about vampires?"

Shellie shook her head. "Not really. I mean, Barry mentioned them in passing, but I'd never met any before now."

"Holy shit!" Tony squeaked. Easing to a sitting position, he leaned against the pillows resting on the headboard. "Have I entered the *Twilight Zone*? I must be dreaming."

Stanton chuckled, grinning. "Naw. Neither of those things." He waggled his brows as a suggestive leer curved his lips. "And it's awesome having a devoted vampire lover. Trust me."

Staring at a clearly happy Stanton for several seconds, Tony tried to wrap his brain around what the man was telling him. Finally, it clicked. "Francois?"

Nodding happily, Stanton didn't seem concerned at all. "Oh, yeah. We're soul mates." With a grin, he finished, "Kinda like you and Kellan and Shellie and Karina."

"Wait, what?" Shellie gasped. "What are you talking about?"

"Jumped ahead a little there, buddy," Jerome stated with a chuckle. He smiled at Shellie. "Did Barry ever talk about mates? Fated mates? Soul mates?"

With a blush staining her cheeks, Shellie nodded. "Once. It was when I filed for divorce." Her brows furrowed as she obviously tried to remember her ex's exact words. "He said something like . . . you aren't my fated mate, so it would have

49

ended soon anyway."

"Asshole," Stanton muttered.

Even though Tony was having a hard time following the discussion, he nodded, too. "Okay, so . . . I really need someone to start at the beginning," Tony pleaded. "There *is* a beginning, right?" Frowning at his brother, he accused, "Not only were you hiding a male lover from me, but now you've been hiding vampires?"

Jerome sighed deeply as he settled onto the side of the bed. "The secret of vampires isn't mine to tell, Tony," he countered. "Their greatest defense against people attacking them is anonymity. They don't normally tell outsiders like me, but Stanton asked for a special exception to be made, since" — he rubbed the back of his neck in discomfort — "I would probably have made trouble if he up and moved without any explanation to me."

"Jerome is like a brother to me," Stanton rumbled, sadness filling his tone. "Better than my own ever was. Plus, living here was closer to you."

"Then why are you all telling me now?" Tony asked, still not following, but he understood the need for secrets. For some reason, the human race was absolutely fantastic at starting wars against anyone different than themselves.

You'd think they'd learn after all these centuries.

"Well, that's where Stanton's beloved comment comes in," Jerome explained slowly. When he rubbed the back of his neck again, Tony knew his brother was uncomfortable with the conversation. "Uhhh . . . how do I begin?"

Stanton didn't seem to have that problem. "It's simple," he claimed. "Paranormals live a really long time, so Fate gives them a person to bond with. A soul mate." He grinned, obviously pleased by what he was saying. "Their lives join together, and the vampire or shifter will spend the rest of their lives pleasing that person." Stanton used his thumb to point at his chest. "Francois is my vampire, completely devoted to me, will never cheat on me, and he works hard to make me happy." With a wink, he added, "And he does a damn fine job of it, so I do everything I can to return the favor."

"By feeding him blood?" Tony blurted out the question without thinking. Except, he did wonder. "All the stories I've heard say vampires drink blood." Then he frowned. "Except, they also say they can only come out at night, and I know there was garlic on the potato wedges served last night."

"Most stories about vampires have a ton of skewed information in them," Jerome told him. Lifting his hand, he began ticking off his fingers. "They don't turn into bats. They don't fly. They aren't allergic to sunlight, garlic, crosses, or holy water."

"Then what *is* true about the stories?" Shellie asked curiously before taking a sip of her drink.

Tony wasn't certain how she could be so calm about everything.

"Well, the blood-drinking, obviously," Jerome replied. "Except, the only time a vampire would drain someone was if they were in battle or if that vampire was a rogue." When Tony's eyebrows furrowed, expressing his confusion, Jerome explained, "Rogue vampires are like human criminals. No society is without their bad apples."

Stanton snorted. "They just do a better job of taking them out because they have to keep their secret from getting out."

Shellie nodded absently. "And you said Karina thinks I'm her . . . soul mate?"

"Right," Jerome confirmed. Reaching over, he patted her hand as he smiled warmly. "The look of joy on her face when you let her hold your hand earlier was something to see."

"Huh," Shellie murmured, cocking her head. Her expression turned a little vacant as she admitted, "I've always been able to admit when I thought a woman was hot or had nice tits or something, but I'd never been attracted enough to actually be interested in trying to figure out if they swung my way." Then she frowned. "How do two women even have sex, since neither of us has a—" Even as Shellie's cheeks took on a dark hue, she made a gesture with her hands indicating a cock and penetration.

Tony wanted to crawl back under the covers. Jerome cleared his throat and stared at the ceiling. Stanton furrowed his brows, appearing confused, as if he were trying to figure it out.

"I'm not going there," Tony finally blurted out. "I won't even try to guess about women and sex."

Jerome cleared his throat before saying, "Why don't you talk to Karina about it?" His smile appeared tight. "She'd be the best to explore that with you, after all, since her main goal in life is to please you, make you happy, and keep you safe."

Shellie hummed as she took on a speculative expression.

Unable to help himself, Tony demanded, "How can you be okay with this?"

Looking confused, she asked, "With what?"

"With . . . with . . ." Tony waved his hand wildly, not understanding how his best friend didn't get it. "Vampires!"

Sighing, Shellie told him, "Tony, I was married to a shifter for almost six years." She shrugged. "A vampire couldn't be much different, and I like the idea of someone being devoted to me." Her look turned troubled as she continued, "Although I think Karina is getting the raw end of the deal. I mean, she's gorgeous with those high firm breasts, slender waist, and lightly muscled limbs." Her expression turned dreamy as she continued, "And her hair and skin? Wow! I would love to—"

"Uh, Shellie," Tony cut in uncomfortably. "I don't really need to know what you want to do with her hair and skin."

Even as Tony spoke, he thought of Kellan's hair and skin.

The man was lightly bronzed, probably from working out-side. He didn't appear to have any blemishes that Tony had noticed, but he would love to explore everywhere. Plus, his dark hair was the perfect length for him to run his fingers through. He could—

Right. I'm not supposed to be thinking about this . . . am I?

Shellie made a rude noise. "As if you're not thinking about something similar about Kellan right now." Her eyes nar-rowed as she pinned him with a knowing look. "I've seen that look in your eyes before, Tony Harsnen."

Even knowing he was busted, he ignored it.

Instead, Tony stated, "And what do you mean Karina is getting the raw end of the deal? You're just as gorgeous as she is." Narrowing his eyes, he added, "And you're smart, kind, and funny."

Rolling her eyes, Shellie claimed, "And my boobs are start-ing to sag from pregnancy growth, and oh, yeah, that's right"—she leaned back and pointed at her rounded belly—"I'm carrying an asshole's shifter son."

"No," Tony immediately countered. "You are carrying *your* shifter son, and he will be amazing and nothing like his father because you're his mother." Straightening, Tony whis-pered, "Oh, damn. Did those words really just come out of my mouth?"

Stanton chuckled. "They sure did." He looked at Shellie. "And Tony's right. There's a bunch of good guys and gals here. Your son will want for nothing and be welcome and ac-cepted." Then Stanton grinned and pointed at Jerome. "And when it comes time to learn how to shift, Cain will teach him."

"Cain?" Tony repeated as he watched Jerome smile and nod. If he'd had a lightbulb in his brain, he figured it would have just switched on. "You said Cain wasn't a vampire. He's a shifter?"

Jerome gripped Tony's calf through the comforter. "Cain is a shifter. He shares his spirit with a red fox and can turn into the animal at will."

Tony blew out a breath as he rested the back of his head against the headboard. "Wow." Lifting his hands to either side of his head, he made an exploding noise. "Mind blown."

"This is actually a good thing," Stanton declared confidently. "Jerome was bummed that he would outlive you by centuries, and now he won't."

"Wait. What?" Tony refocused on Stanton. "What's that mean?"

"We did mention that paranormals live a very long time," Jerome reminded him. "Fate isn't going to give a paranormal their fated match, then allow the human in the paring to die after fifty or seventy years."

Tony felt his heartrate begin to speed up again, but he did his best to breathe through the rising panic. "Then what happens?"

"When a human bonds with their shifter or vampire, their life threads entwine," Jerome explained. "You'll live as long as Kellan." His brows furrowed as he admitted, "I don't actually know how old the vampire is. My guess would be a couple of centuries, seeing as he's the second-in-command of the coven."

"Second-in-command?" Tony rubbed his hands over his face. "Meaning, he normally gets what he wants, right?"

Jerome's dark brows drew together. "Sure, Tony, but you need to remember one thing about Kellan."

Warily, Tony asked, "What's that?"

Pinning him with a serious gaze, Jerome told him, "To Kellan, you are a gift, something to be treasured and cared for and pleased in every way he can think of." He smiled as he added, "He will never force you, and he'll give you all the time you need to decide what you want."

Even as Tony nodded, he wondered how he could figure out what he wanted when he was more confused than ever.

CHAPTER EIGHT

"Hi, Kellan."

Upon hearing the deep voice, Kellan turned away from the view of the ranch and rested his butt against the railing. He arched one brow as he watched the Horseman of War walk silently across the plank decking toward him. The huge black creature's horns nearly touched the roof.

"Hello, War," Kellan greeted, dipping his chin just a smidge in deference to the horseman. "How can I help you?"

Even though War was one of Monte's lovers, he didn't interact with him much. The horseman had a very busy job of managing hundreds of demons, just as each of his three brothers did—Death, Pestilence, and Famine. Each answered to the gods while completing tasks for the Moirai—the three fates—and were charged with keeping the balance between humans and the earth on Kellan's plane.

"It's not what you can do for me," War replied enigmatically. "It's what I can do for you."

Meeting the horseman's red-eyed gaze, Kellan tapped his beer bottle on his jeans-clad thigh. "I'm sorry, War. I don't follow you."

War grinned, showing off plenty of pointy teeth. "Before I got together with Monte, you offered me advice." He winked. "I'm here to return the favor."

Kellan had completely forgotten about that. Everyone had recognized that War wanted Monte, but his buddy had been resistant, to say the least. Some prejudices died hard, even when they were born of misunderstandings. Kellan had essentially told War to stop *talking* about how he could please Monte and to start *doing it*, instead.

Of course, then Monte had run across Xerxes, his fated prairie dog shifter beloved, had nearly died, and made a deal with War to bond both to him in order to live. Fortunately, it had all worked out, and the trio were a fantastic thruple.

Still—"I'm not certain how you can help, War," Kellan admitted. "Tony seems to be having a hard enough time accepting vampires and shifters. I'm not certain he's ready to be introduced to demons or horsemen, yet." Lifting his free hand in placation, Kellan added, "No offense."

War tipped his head back and laughed, the sound booming across the still evening.

Kellan waited him out, smirking at the male.

Finally, grinning widely, War wrapped his huge red wings around himself and eased onto one of the rocking chairs. He folded his hands over his chiseled abdominals before telling him, "I'm talking about advice." With a wink, War told him, "I have no intention of freaking out your human."

Crossing to another rocker, Kellan relaxed into it. "Sorry. My mind is pretty scattered." With a sigh, he added, "I should have known that wasn't what you meant, War."

War shrugged his huge shoulders. "No worries."

"And I'm happy to accept any advice," Kellan added before taking a swig of his beer, downing the last of it.

Lifting his hands, palms up, and whispering a few harsh words in the demon tongue, War caused two wooden mugs to appear. "It's honeyed mead from the demon realm," he cautioned as he held one out to Kellan. "So, strong, even for a vampire."

"Thank you," Kellan stated, accepting the glass and the warning. "And any advice is welcome."

"Well, you reminded me to do something that pleased

Monte, not just to talk about it," War stated before taking a swig of his drink.

Kellan nodded, recalling, before taking a tentative sip of his own drink. The beverage was warm and a little sweet. It flowed smoothly and pleasantly across his tongue.

Very nice.

Even as Kellan recalled War's words, he took a slightly larger drink.

"Well, if you want me to read his thoughts and find out what would please him, I can do that for you."

Fighting back his initial reaction—to growl at War's offer to invade his beloved's privacy—Kellan cleared his throat instead. Otherwise, he would have been snarling when he spoke. Instead, he took a few seconds to shake his head slowly.

"As nice as it would be to have it that simple for me," Kellan began slowly, doing his best to be polite, "I don't want you to do that. If Tony found out, he could consider it an invasion of his privacy."

War nodded, stroking his smooth chin. "I see." Then he chuckled. "I guess you'll have to do it the old-fashioned way."

"Uhhhh, what way is that?" Kellan asked, curious as to what War would consider old-fashioned. After all, the horseman had been around since . . . forever.

Snorting, War stated, "You're going to have to ask his friends and family."

Kellan lifted his hand to his mouth, fighting back a laugh. Only War would think that asking instead of reading someone's mind was old-fashioned. The horseman had a funny way of looking at the world.

"Oh, but I did notice him in the window earlier this afternoon," War told him absently. "He was watching Kase and Raphael riding in the arena, and there was this look of longing on his face." War snapped his fingers. "Hey, you should take him horseback riding."

Kellan nodded slowly, liking that idea. "I just need to figure out how to convince him to go somewhere alone with me," he admitted, wondering how long it would be before he could do that. "He's refused to come out of his room all day."

"So take Jerome, Stanton, and their partners," War offered before taking another long drink. Kellan remained quiet, musing over that, giving War time to add, "Then the others can ditch you both for some reason, and you can have him all to yourself."

"Uh . . . Tony will know he's been manipulated," Kellan pointed out, concerned about how Tony would take that. "He could be upset."

War shrugged. "So? He'll get over it." As he rose to his feet, he pointed out, "The human in the pairing feels the pull, too. Take advantage of that." As War began heading toward the porch steps, he called, "Now you just need to find out what your man would like for a picnic."

Before Kellan could call out a thank you, between one step and the next, War disappeared.

Kellan shook his head as he thought about War's advice. The horseman wasn't wrong. He needed alone time with Tony in a neutral environment.

Could the allure of horseback riding be strong enough to get Tony out of his bedroom?

Taking a swig of his mead, Kellan wondered about his other problem. He knew where he could get answers to that, though. Rising to his feet, he headed back into the house.

Kellan headed to the family room first. Spotting Shellie and Karina in the corner, sitting close and talking, a pang of jealousy twisted his gut. The pregnant woman seemed to be taking the whole fated beloved thing so much better than Tony.

Of course, that could be because she had been married to a shifter.

Why a shifter would marry a woman who wasn't his fated mate, Kellan would never understand.

But Fate guided Shellie to Tony to help me. I'm certain of it.

Even though the pair appeared very cozy, Kellan headed their way. Karina spotted him before he could overhear any of their whispered words. She smiled at him, joy shining in her brown eyes.

Considering how close they sat and how they held hands, Kellan figured Karina had a reason to be happy.

"My apologies for intruding, Karina, Shellie." Kellan smiled at them both. "But I have a few questions and need some advice."

Shellie's smile held an obvious touch of commiseration. "You mean, like the best way to get Tony out of his room and willing to spend some time with you?"

Kellan chuckled depreciatively as he nodded. "Exactly."

Indicating a nearby chair, Shellie asked, "Will you join us? I'll help any way I can." She sighed. "I don't know you, but I know Tony deserves to be happy, so if you're it, and Fate seems to think so, well" — then she scowled and pointed at him — "but don't you think I won't be watching you."

Karina gasped and grabbed Shellie's hand, making her lower it. "Beloved," she gasped. The female vampire peered at Kellan, concern written all over her face.

When Karina opened her mouth, probably to apologize for Shellie, Kellan waved her away. "I understand being protective of a friend," he told Shellie with a nod. "Believe me. His happiness is the only thing I care about." Then Kellan rolled his eyes and admitted, "Well, along with his safety and the fact that he stays by my side. Call me selfish, if you will."

Shellie shook her head. "That's not selfish at all." After reaching over and resting her hand on Karina's thigh, she smiled. "So, how can I help? Do you have a plan?"

Nodding slowly, Kellan told her, "War noticed Tony in the window looking toward the arena. Does he ride?"

With the invention of vehicles, Kellan knew that many humans never bothered to learn the skill.

Her blue eyes lit up as Shellie nodded. "He does! Why didn't I think of that?" Then she rolled her eyes and grumbled, "Damn pregnancy hormones messing with my brain. If I weren't pregnant, I would have thought of that. I—"

As Karina hushed Shellie's self-deprecating words with a peck to her lips, Kellan drank the last of his mead and set the mug on a nearby coffee table. Then he returned his focus to the couple and pressed, "So Tony does ride?"

Shellie refocused on him, nodding enthusiastically. "He does. He loves it, too. In Detroit, he would head to the country a couple of times a month to rent a horse and trail ride at a stable out there." Her cheeks glowed as she warmed to the subject. "He asked me to go a few times, but I only went once. I had no idea they would be so big up close." As if realizing what she was admitting, she focused on Karina. "Sorry. I, um . . . I don't think I'll be able to ride with you."

Karina smiled warmly at Shellie. "Maybe that'll change in a few decades," she offered, tucking a loose strand of hair behind Shellie's ear. "And if it doesn't, that's fine, too."

Shellie smiled back, her happiness at the response clear.

Kellan discreetly cleared his throat, redrawing their attention to him. "Soooo, what about Jerome and Stanton. I know Stanton is learning, but I can't remember about Jerome."

While Jerome called the ranch home, sharing a room in the bunkhouse with Cain, both men worked in town—Jerome in construction and Cain as a deputy.

"According to Tony, Jerome rides, but I couldn't tell you how long it's been," Shellie told him. "I bet once he hears you want to take Tony out, he'll make sure everyone goes. Him and Stanton both."

Kellan was counting on it.

"Okay." Kellan rested his forearms on his thighs and leaned toward the pregnant woman, pleased to have an ally in his plotting. "What about the perfect picnic. Has he ever talked about that?"

Shellie's smile turned evil as her eyes narrowed. Tapping her forefinger on her bottom lip, she hummed thoughtfully. Focusing on him, Shellie smirked.

"Oh, I know just the thing."

As Kellan listened, he felt his gut warm in anticipation.

CHAPTER NINE

"I'm not taking no for an answer," Jerome declared, frowning at Tony. "Put the damn boots on, plop the hat on your head, and come with me."

"I'm not going out there," Tony stated, shaking his head. "There are vampires out there."

Duh!

Jerome growled at Tony, crossing his arms over his head. "Oh, I see what's going on here."

"It's about damn time," Tony responded, relief flooding him. "We need to leave. Where's Shellie and Stanton?"

No way did he want to leave his friends behind.

Scoffing, Jerome stated, "Stanton is waiting at the barn with Francois for our horseback ride. Shellie is with Karina, touring the foaling barn, trying to get over her fear of horses by petting cute little babies."

Gaping, Tony cried, "You allowed Shellie to go somewhere with Karina alone?" Fear coiled in Tony's gut. "How could you?"

Jerome clenched his jaw a second, his eyes narrowing. "Shellie is a grown woman," he pointed out. "I don't *allow* her to do anything. If she wants to spend time with someone, I'm not going to stop her."

"But she could be hurt." Tony leaped to his feet as he grabbed at a couple of his braids and tugged. "You don't know what that vampire could do to her."

Lifting his gaze to the ceiling as if silently begging for patience, Jerome let out a long sigh. When he refocused on Tony, he was surprised to see the angry expression on his features.

"What?" Tony stopped in his tracks, confused about why his brother would be upset with him.

"I didn't realize you'd turned out to be so racist."

Tony gaped, shocked upon hearing Jerome's words. "What?" He shook his head. "I'm not racist."

"Yes, you are."

"No, I'm not."

"You really are."

Tony suddenly felt as if he were twelve, arguing with his brother in such a way. Still, he countered, "No, I'm really *not*."

"You won't go out of your room because you refuse to interact with vampires." Jerome stated the obvious, only to ruin it by saying, "That's racist. You're racist against vampires."

"B-But . . ." Tony tried to figure out why Jerome didn't get it. "They're not *human*." No matter how hot Kellan was, how attracted he was to the man, he had to keep that fact in the forefront of his mind. "Kellan's not human."

"No, he's not," Jerome agreed. "Kellan is a vampire. A being that's a different *race*." He accentuated the word. "By you refusing to interact with any of them, being willing to learn about them, to think about their point of view, even if you don't share it, you're the very definition of racist."

Tony didn't want to believe Jerome's words as he eased back onto his comforter. "But they're dangerous," he whispered. "You said they were stronger and faster, had heightened reflexes," he pointed out, referring to one of their many conversations over the last two days. Meeting Jerome's narrow-eyed gaze, Tony pointed out, "They could hurt us any time they wanted to."

Jerome cocked an eyebrow. "Did any of them do anything remotely painful before you found out they were vampires and hid away like a dick?"

Glaring, Tony bounced back to his feet. "Hey, that's not

fair." He pointed at his brother. "I didn't know what they were then."

"You didn't know what they were?"

Tony nodded. "Yeah."

"You didn't know they were willing to help you with no questions asked, just because you are my brother?"

Frowning, Tony muttered, "No, I knew that."

"Or give you a roof over your head, a bed to sleep in, and food for your belly?"

His belly clenched with uncertainty. "Um, no. I realized that, too."

"So, the only thing that changed was the fact that they like to bite their lovers."

Tony suddenly had the image of Kellan biting someone—someone other than him—pop into his mind. Angry at the jealousy he felt every time he thought about it, he grumbled, "I bet they don't restrict it to the bedroom."

"Many lovers don't restrict their bed-play to the actual bedroom," Jerome pointed out.

Feeling his face heat, Tony couldn't believe he was discussing this with his brother. "Damn it. What do you want from me?"

Jerome shrugged one shoulder before reaching out and gripping Tony's bicep. "I want you out of this bedroom. I've allowed you to hide for two days, and that's long enough." Resting his second hand on Tony's opposite shoulder, his brother peered deep into his eyes. "Tell me what's really going on with you. I've never seen you act like this before."

Swallowing hard, Tony tried to get some, any, moisture into his suddenly too-dry throat. "I—" He swallowed, trying again. Knowing he needed to trust his brother, he whispered, "I'm scared."

"Of what, Tony?" Jerome asked softly. "You have to know that no one here would hurt you."

Tony jerked his head in a hard shake. "Not that."

"Then what?" Jerome pressed. Tapping Tony's temple lightly, he asked, "What's going on up here?"

Unable to meet Jerome's searching gaze, Tony admitted, "I'm scared of how my mind and body react to Kellan. I don't even have to be around him. I—"

Just thinking about him caused a surge of arousal to heat him from the inside out.

"Ahhhh," Jerome murmured, a knowing smile curving his lips. His dark eyes actually twinkled. "You know, the attraction is normal between mates, and he would never take advantage of that fact." Smiling, Jerome reminded him, "You are a gift from the gods, from Fate. He wants to please you in every way possible."

Tony groaned, jerking away from his brother. "I so don't want to talk about sex with you."

"When did you turn into such a prude?" Jerome teased.

"Now I'm a prude, too?" Tony asked incredulously.

Jerome grinned broadly, resting his hands on his hips. "If the shoe fits." He shrugged. "I would have thought you'd appreciate being able to talk about gay sex with your brother." Waggling his eyebrows, Jerome added, "Especially now that I have experience and can actually offer knowledgeable advice."

"Oh, god." Tony clapped both hands over his face, hiding. Too bad that didn't stop him from hearing his brother's voice.

"For example, I now know exactly how different size vibrators feel, and can give you advice on choosing—"

"Stop!" Tony cried, lifting his hands in placation. "For the love of god, stop. I'll go horseback riding with you just to get you to shut up!"

Tipping his head back, Jerome laughed. "Sure, sure. Then maybe I should remind you not to let your lover pound your ass too hard if you plan to ride the next day," he warned. "It

could make sitting in the saddle a little uncomfortable. Also —
"

"Just *stop*," Tony whined, grabbing the boots Jerome had brought him and yanking them on. "I don't want to think about you getting your—" He stopped speaking and shuddered at the thought.

Maybe it was because his brother had partially raised him, but thinking of him having sex gave him the heebity-jeebies. *Ugh!*

After finishing with the boots, Tony grabbed the hat and hustled from the room. A laughing Jerome followed him.

"If I'd known talking about sex would have this reaction, I would have done it yesterday," his brother teased.

Tony ignored him, hustling down the hall away from the man. Unfortunately, his brother had longer legs and had no trouble keeping up with him. Jerome guided him toward the back of the house as he kept talking.

"Oh, hey," Jerome continued. "Cain and I found this amazing waterproof lube perfect for use in the shower. We normally buy a six-pack at a time," he told him. "I bet we have an unopened bottle. I'll grab it after the ride."

"Why the hell would I need — "

Tony's words died in his throat. He'd just stepped out the back door and had peered across the yard. He spotted Kellan, Cain, Stanton, and Francois standing around the hitching posts. Six horses were saddled, and Tony realized he wasn't going with just his brother and friend.

His gut twisted in a mixture of fear and desire as he took in Kellan's tall, strong, sexy frame.

"Relax," Jerome rumbled into his ear. "He would never hurt you." When Tony tore his focus away from the handsome vampire and looked at Jerome, his brother smiled in reassurance. "You're everything to him. He wants to please you more than you could possibly imagine."

"Is that what happened between you and Cain?" Tony

whispered, realizing he'd never actually heard the unedited version of how his brother had hooked up with the shifter. "Because you're mates?"

"Being mates just happened to help us bounce over the humps of him being engaged and me having never really wanting a guy," Jerome told him, urging him to begin walking down the stairs. "We're the ones that still have to make concessions and work at the relationship. That includes communication." Squeezing Tony's shoulder, Jerome whispered into his ear, "When you're alone with him, be honest about what's been bothering you. Okay?"

"When I'm alone?" Tony suddenly had the feeling that he was being set up.

That sensation was reaffirmed when his brother winked at him.

The first hour of the ride went smoothly.

It had been a couple of months since he'd been on a horse. Once Barry had started harassing Shellie, Tony hadn't wanted to be that far away from her. He took his time reminding his muscles how to move with his mount. Kellan stayed close, but not too close, and pointed out various features of the ranch.

Tony had to admit that the place was stunning. They rode through rolling hills, sprawling meadows, copses of trees, and even past a few smaller ponds. The conversation stayed light. Jerome and Stanton talked about work. Francois discussed upcoming dishes for the hands with Kellan. Even Cain shared a couple of funny stories about working as a deputy in a small town.

Finally, they stopped at the side of a lake that abutted both a forest and a meadow.

Cain stopped his horse and swung from the saddle. "I wanna stretch my fox's legs." He grinned as he waggled his brows. "Interested in a game of chase, Jerome?"

Jerome chuckled huskily as he swung from the saddle. "What do I get if I catch you?"

Giving Jerome a look that could only be called hungry, Cain replied, "Anything you want."

"I like the sound of that," Jerome replied as they both tied their horses to nearby trees. He grinned as he began walking backward in the direction Cain was already heading. With a wave, tugging his shirt from his torso, Jerome called, "We'll catch up with you in a bit."

Then his brother turned and jogged after his lover.

"Hey, I know where we are," Stanton claimed as he peered around, not at all concerned about Jerome running around with a fox. "There's a clay bed on the other side of this lake that I really want to check out. I think I could use the consistency for pottery."

"You do pottery?" Tony asked slowly as he swung from his horse's back. After all, everyone else was, too.

Stanton nodded. "Just dabbling in it, really."

Tony shrugged. "I'll check it out with you." Not that he knew anything about clay or pottery.

"Uh, actually." Stanton shifted from foot to foot, his gaze straying to where Francois tied up his horse near the others. "I was gonna have Francois suck my dick, soooo do you mind staying here?"

"U-Uh, yeah," Tony instantly replied, having never heard anyone speak quite so bluntly.

Stanton's grin was blinding. "Thanks."

Francois chuckled as he took Stanton's hand. "You are such a sweet talker, my beloved."

"You like sucking my dick," Stanton replied, his voice growing quiet as they moved away.

"Zat I do."

Then they were too far away to hear.

Clearing his throat, Tony glanced at Kellan, then around

the area. "Um, uh, d-did you want to g-go back to the r-ranch?" he stuttered, rubbing his sweaty palm on his jeans. "I'm sure you have things to do."

"Currently, the only thing I have to do is visit with you while we wait for our friends to get done with their . . . playful activities." The vampire untied saddlebags from his horse. "I have a few things to occupy us while we wait."

Tony snapped his attention to Kellan, watching him spread a deep blue blanket on the grass near the lake's edge while still under the shade of the trees.

"Did you set this up?" The question popped out of Tony's mouth before he could think better of it.

Without missing a beat, Kellan smiled and replied, "Of course I did."

What? Holy shit!

CHAPTER TEN

K ellan saw the fear flash through Tony's eyes even before the acrid scent reached his nostrils. As much as he wanted to take his beloved into his arms and soothe him, he knew his touch wouldn't be welcome . . . yet.

Gotta earn his trust first.

Turning away from Tony, Kellan placed the saddlebags on the blanket. He kicked off his boots and set them to the side. Then he tossed his hat on top of them. After tugging his shirts from the waistband of his pants, Kellan dropped to sit cross-legged on the blanket.

When no sound other than the quick thud of Tony's heart-beat reached him, he wondered if his beloved was about to flee. He turned and found his human exactly where he'd left him. Tony clutched the reins of his mount in one hand while rubbing the palm of his other on his thigh.

"Tony, will you join me?" Kellan asked softly. He knew better than to reach out a hand.

For several long seconds, Tony just continued to stand there.

Kellan waited patiently, knowing he could do little else.

Finally, Tony led his horse to a tree, unhooked the lead from the saddle, and tied the animal with the others. He turned to face Kellan, met his gaze, and paused. After Tony swallowed so hard his Adam's apple bobbed, he began to walk slowly toward him.

Taking that as a win, Kellan turned his attention to unpack-ing the snacks he'd brought. He pulled out a bottle of red wine — Malbec, as recommended by Shellie — as well as a couple of metal cups. After popping the cork on the bottle, Kellan poured a bit into both cups. He slid a reusable cork into the bottle and set it in the grass.

Then Kellan began removing containers from the saddlebags. He also had plastic plates and silverware, although he didn't have to use the latter. Finally, he drew out a bottle of whipping cream.

Kellan watched Tony kneel several feet before him. For a second, he remained there stiffly. Finally, as if coming to a decision, he eased to the left, settling more comfortably on the blanket.

"So, you asked my brother and friends to help you get me out here."

While it wasn't a question, Kellan nodded anyway. "I hoped enjoying an activity you liked as well as the fresh air might help you calm down a little," he told his beloved. Then he held out a cup of wine. "And a drink and snacks are always a great way to break the ice."

Tony took the cup and, to Kellan's delight, took a sip. His beloved hummed softly as he swallowed. "One of my favorite Malbecs," he murmured, staring into the drink.

Kellan took a sip of his own before setting it aside. "It is a good vintage," he conceded. "I'd never had it before."

Nodding, Tony remained quiet as Kellan opened the plastic containers. He revealed egg salad finger sandwiches cut into triangles as well as fresh, crisp potato wedges. From the scent of it, there was a bit of garlic added into them. Finally, there was a container of fruit containing apple slices, grape halves, quartered strawberries, and pineapple slices. All of them were cut into the perfect size to dip into the cream before eating.

"Shellie planned this, didn't she?"

Lifting his gaze from everything, Kellan rested his hands

on his knees. "She did plan the meal," he conceded. "Yes." Cocking his head, he asked, "Should I have chosen something else for our first date?"

Scoffing, Tony shook his head. "No. This is perfect," he told him softly. A smile even teased at the corners of his lips. Meeting his gaze, Tony told him, "Shellie and I have discussed what would make the perfect first dates on a few occasions. This is one I came up with."

Kellan smiled back at him. "I'm glad to hear it."

"Are you doing this just because of Fate and the whole *beloved* thing?"

Although Kellan had expected the question eventually— he knew it was a point that humans often got hung up on— he hadn't thought Tony would ask it first thing. Still, he'd vowed to be honest with his beloved. Squaring his shoulders, he pinned a firm gaze on his human.

"Even if the answer was yes, would that be so wrong?"

"I—" Tony snapped his mouth shut and cocked his head.

Kellan realized he'd surprised his beloved. "Not what you expected?"

Tony rubbed one cheek, telling Kellan that it probably felt warm to the human, even if he couldn't see the man blush due to his dark skin. "Actually . . . yeah."

"When I made these plans," Kellan began, picking up a sandwich before holding out the container to Tony, who took one, too. "I promised I would answer honestly, even if it made things difficult. I don't want any falsehoods between us." Then Kellan took a bite and waited.

"So you don't really have a choice in who you spend the rest of your life with?"

Watching Tony eat something he'd provided, even if only by giving it to him, warmed Kellan from the inside out. He smiled. Then he recalled Tony's question.

"It's not like that," Kellan claimed.

"Then what's it like?" Tony asked before taking another bite.

"Fate would not pair two people that could not make a go of it." Kellan believed that with all his heart. "Just like any two people will have problems and need to sort out certain aspects of their relationship, Fate matches people who are compatible." Deciding to ask a question of his own, Kellan asked, "If I weren't a vampire, would you dismiss me out of hand?"

"I-It's not that," Tony claimed, although his scent turned acrid with deception, and he shoved the last of his sandwich into his mouth, probably to stop himself from saying more.

Kellan finished his own sandwich, uncertain how to draw the truth from Tony. He grabbed the bottle of fry sauce and poured a healthy dollop onto the lid from the potato wedges. Then he grabbed one and dipped it into the sauce.

Before taking a bite, Kellan decided to try, "I'm worried that *is* the case, even if you're not certain of it, yet."

"It's not that you're a vampire," Tony claimed again, grabbing his own potato wedge as well as a second sandwich. "It's the . . ." He nibbled his bottom lip, grimacing.

"It's the . . . biting?" Kellan guessed.

Plenty of humans had hang-ups with the idea of drinking blood. He'd never actually understood it, either. After all, the first thing most people did when they cut their finger was to stick it in their mouth to soothe the sting.

Humans are so weird sometimes.

"No, I don't care about blood," Tony countered, waving the potato wedge he'd just dipped in fry sauce. A drip of the stuff went flying, but Tony appeared too pre-occupied to notice. "I'm afraid of my responses to you," he blurted out. "I've never responded to anyone as viscerally as I have with you, and it scares the shit out of me."

"Oh," Kellan whispered.

That's unexpected.

Kellan grabbed a napkin and wiped his hands as he tried

to think of a way to assuage his beloved's fears. Taking a chance, after he'd tossed the napkin to the blanket, he reached out. Gently, Kellan took Tony's hand between his own.

"The desire between a vampire and his beloved will always be there," Kellan started slowly, massaging his lover. "The desire to touch, to kiss, and to hold, *that* will never go away," he warned. "Whenever you walk into a room, I'll want you next to me so I can put my arm around you."

"So, this isn't one-sided?" Tony asked slowly. "This need to touch." He teased the fingertips of his free hand over the back of one of Kellan's. "This isn't because I'm not the paranormal, and Fate is messing with my hormones to get me to do as she's decided."

Kellan hummed as he leaned forward and brought Tony's fingers to his lips. Licking lightly, he tasted the salt from the potato wedges he'd been eating. Gathering enough self-control to answer, Kellan lowered his hand and threaded their fingers together.

"She does do that. I won't lie," Kellan admitted. "But you're not alone in facing that desire." He cleared his throat, doing his best to concentrate. "Once we complete our bond, this driving need for sex will ease somewhat, although our desire for each other will never diminish completely." Seeing Tony's surprised expression, Kellan quickly added, "And if you want to wait, we'll do so for as long as you wish."

"What about your need for blood?"

Damn. He's perceptive.

Licking his lips, Kellan sighed deeply. "Well, I would drink bagged blood for as long as you needed to accept me."

"But you *do* plan for me to accept you, accept *this*," Tony used his free hand to indicate between them. "Eventually."

"Yes." Kellan allowed his desire to enter his expression as he swept his gaze over Tony. "You are my beloved, after all, Tony, so I'll do everything I can to sweep you off your feet and prove that you'll be happy here with me."

To Kellan's disappointment, Tony pulled his hand away. He was about to open his mouth and ask why when Tony kicked off his boots. He tossed them to where Kellan's were. Then his hat joined them.

"You know what happened when Shellie moved in with me?"

Unable to even guess, Kellan shook his head. He was too busy watching Tony unbutton his flannel shirt to gather enough brain cells to guess anyway. It looked like his beloved was undressing, but that couldn't possibly be right.

"I stopped having sex because I was too busy making certain she was getting over her asshole ex."

Kellan yanked his attention to Tony's face, unable to stop his low growl. "Please do not speak of past lovers to me," he requested. "I find I'm too possessive to think of you with another, no matter how ridiculous that seems."

Tony chuckled as he rose up onto his knees. "Not what I meant, but I'll respect that if you do the same."

Then Tony pulled his flannel shirt over his head, revealing a tank top underneath. The white of the fabric accentuated his beloved's dark skin, making his mouth water for a taste. He reached out, touching the soft material, feeling the firmness of the skin beneath.

"Okay," Kellan mumbled, distracted.

Reaching out, Tony gripped Kellan's hand. At first, he thought he would push him away. To his pleasure, he discovered he was wrong.

Tony lifted his shirt halfway up his abdominals and urged Kellan to place his hand on him. Eager to please, he began exploring his soon-to-be lover's smooth skin. The heady aroma of his beloved's arousal filled his nostrils, going straight to his head — both of them — and he nearly missed his beloved's next words.

"What I'm saying," Tony murmured huskily. "Is that I've

been celibate for over seven months. I want you to end my dry spell . . . right now."

Groaning, Kellan grabbed Tony's waist and held him in a firm grip. "If we do this, I'll claim you, Tony," he warned, searching his beloved's gaze. "I won't be able to stop myself."

Smirking, Tony murmured, "Stanton says getting bitten will make me orgasm."

"It will." Kellan would never cause his beloved pain.

"Soooo, you'll get me off a couple of times then, huh?"

Kellan spotted the challenge in Tony's eyes and grinned. "Oh, yes, my beloved." *Challenge accepted.* "How would you like me to take you?"

"What if I want to take you?" Tony knee-walked closer, placing a hand on Kellan's chest and pushing.

While Kellan could have resisted, there was nothing he wanted more than to lie with his beloved. Still, it had been a long damn time since he'd bottomed. He swallowed hard, then nodded as he sprawled on the blanket.

"If that is your wish, my beloved," Kellan told his human as he grabbed the hem of his tank top. Lifting it, he added, "My ass is yours any time you wish it."

For his beloved, Kellan would do anything.

When Tony's face reappeared, a wide grin curved his lips. His eyes sparkled, and he even shook his head once as he levered over him. "You would let me take you even though it's clearly not your favorite." Before Kellan managed an answer, Tony added, "Your expression said it all." Then he winked. "Good thing I'm pretty much a total bottom boy. It's rare that I want to top."

Kellan realized he'd just been played. "Minx!"

Then Kellan grabbed Tony and rolled them.

CHAPTER ELEVEN

Tony laughed as he suddenly found himself the one on the bottom. While he had every intention of riding Kellan soon, he enjoyed the play beforehand. It was all part of the fun . . . fun he couldn't remember having in years.

Shutting down that line of thought, Tony focused on Kellan. There was no place for past lovers in his mind while enjoying his time with the man who would be his forever. He didn't know how that forever would play out, yet, but after letting go of his fears, he wanted it to start as soon as possible.

As Kellan got to his knees and yanked off his own shirts, Tony was still trying to wrap his mind around all the vampire's hard work. He'd planned a damn perfect date for him. Then he'd gone and been as honest as possible, expressing how he, too, was affected by everything between them.

Tony respected him for that, and he couldn't wait for what other layers the man had.

"Refocus on me, Tony," Kellan crooned into his ear as he rubbed one hand down his side, teasing at the skin along his ribcage. "Did I do something wrong?"

"Just dwelling on how you've done everything right," Tony admitted as he began rubbing his palms up and down Kellan's strong torso. "I didn't mean to make you think I wasn't appreciating you."

While Tony had never wrestled a day in his life, he knew a few moves. Wrapping one leg around Kellan's thighs, he grabbed his upper arms and twisted. With a push from his other leg, he rolled them back over.

Kellan hissed and peered to the right.

Tony followed his gaze and spotted the can of whipping cream. "Mmmm, I'll definitely be using this later," he crooned, moving the can to the side. "And let's get the rest of this out of the way." With a wink while sliding some of the containers out of the way, Tony claimed, "I like a little food-play as much as the next man, but I also like to choose when and where."

Chuckling, Kellan nodded agreement. "Now, I think we're both overdressed." Then he quickly undid Tony's fly.

As Tony reached for the button of Kellan's jeans to return the favor, he froze. "Um, do you have lube?"

Tony watched as Kellan's cheeks took on just a hint of pink. "I did bring some, as presumptuous as it was." He pointed at the saddlebags. "The left one."

"Definitely presumptuous," Tony agreed as he leaned over and fished out the tube. As he returned to his position straddling Kellan's thighs, he told the man, "But I appreciate it all the same."

Kellan smiled up at him, his brown eyes full of relief. "I'm glad." Gripping Tony's waist, he teased his thumbs along the waistband of his underwear. "When a vampire finds his or her beloved, we always want to be prepared to pleasure the other half of our soul."

"Suddenly, I find it so sexy to be called that," Tony admitted, his cock throbbing behind his underwear. It could also have been the way Kellan scraped his nails over his hipbones.

Either way worked for him.

"I-I have a funny feeling this first round is going to be quick," Tony muttered, rolling off the vampire to make swift work of shucking his jeans, underwear, and socks. When Tony returned his attention to Kellan, he saw that the man was blissfully naked, sprawled out in all his delicious, well-muscled glory. "Damn," Tony mumbled, straddling him once more. "There's not a bit of you that isn't perfect."

"I could say the same about you," Kellan rumbled, sliding his palms up and down Tony's torso. "Your dark skin is absolute perfection."

Tony shook his head as he located the lube he'd dropped in his rush to get naked. "Not really."

Because Tony didn't want to hear Kellan counter him, he grabbed the hard rod jutting from his new lover's groin and squeezed. Predictably, Kellan groaned and bucked into his grip. He allowed the hard, smooth, maybe eight-inch cock to slide through his hold.

"*This* is absolute perfection," Tony countered, continuing to jack him. "I can't wait to feel it plowing my ass."

Groaning, Kellan muttered through gritted teeth, "Damn it, Tony. I'm supposed to be pleasuring you."

With a laugh, Tony released him, drawing a dismayed moan from Kellan. He quickly popped the cap on the lube and drizzled a healthy dollop onto not only the fingers of his right hand, but also Kellan's jutting shaft. Enjoying Kellan's hiss, he used a thumb to close it before dropping it aside.

Then Tony grabbed Kellan again. "Is that a vampire rule?" he teased as he began jacking the man again. At the same time, Tony rose up on his knees and slid his index finger into his rectum. Fighting past his breathlessness, Tony continued, "The vampire has to do all the pleasuring?"

Grunting, busy rocking his hips into Tony's hold, it took Kellan a few seconds to answer. "Yes," he replied breathlessly. "I'm the fucking vampire second." Kellan peeled his fingers from the blanket beneath him and grabbed Tony's waist. "I'm in charge."

"Keep telling yourself that," Tony quipped with a laugh. "I'm a power bottom."

As Tony spoke, he twisted his hand on the way up Kellan's cock. Then he swiped over his head, flicking the man's piss slit with one fingernail. At the same time, he rubbed his frenulum with his thumb.

Tony watched with satisfaction as Kellan groaned and shuddered beneath him. While his fingers were tight on Tony's hips, they weren't too tight. He also began rocking into Tony's hold again, giving him time to start stretching himself in earnest, adding a second, then a third finger.

"Oh, fuck yeah!" Kellan growled, his eyes narrowing. "Next time, I get to watch," he declared even as he rubbed his palms up and teased over Tony's nipples.

Sparks shot through Tony's chest, causing a jolt to shoot through him. The involuntary movement meant he inadvertently nudged his prostate. Blissful tingles of fire shot up his rectum, settling in his balls.

"Oh damn," Tony whined. "Need you."

"Do you have three fingers in you, Tony?" Kellan asked roughly. His big hands easily gripped Tony's torso while continuing to flick his thumbs back and forth over his nipples. "I'm thick. I don't want to hurt you."

"I noticed." Tony gave the shaft he'd been working a pointed squeeze. "Got my hand on you, after all."

As Kellan hissed through clenched teeth, his irises began to bleed to red.

Seeing that, Tony froze in surprise.

"Easy," Kellan crooned, sliding his hands down to gently grip Tony's dick to jack him lightly, distracting him. "It's normal. It doesn't mean I'm going to hurt you."

Blowing out a breath, Tony pushed away his surprise. "Just caught me off guard," he admitted as he pulled his fingers free of his channel. "Yes to the three fingers. I'm ready for you."

Tony started easing forward, then froze once more. "Condom?"

"Gods, we suck at conversation," Kellan mumbled with a

rough, broken laugh. "No condom. Paranormal, remember?"

Seeing the stark need stretching Kellan's features and feeling the desire in his own body, Tony decided to take him at his word. "Okay."

As Kellan helped move Tony into position, he added, "Can't bond us unless I spill in you, Tony." His gaze grew serious. "Thank you for your trust."

Tony positioned Kellan's slicked cock at his prepared hole and smiled at his lover. "You're welcome. Thank you for your patience."

"You're welcome," Kellan repeated. Then his grin turned feral. "Now, out of patience."

Kellan thrust up.

Between the vampire's grip on Tony's hips and the strength of his pump, his erection sank balls deep inside him. He gasped, feeling the burn of the unexpected stretch. Pushing out, he refused to tense up, knowing Kellan would feel it.

As Kellan relaxed his hips back to the blanket, he took Tony with him. He found himself sitting on the vampire's lap. To Tony's pleasure, he noticed they were both panting and sweating.

"Oh, fuck, my beloved," Kellan ground out. "You feel so wonderful. Beyond compare." His words came out slurred and rough. "Never knew what I was missing." Then Kellan fixed a surprisingly clear gaze on him, even though his irises remained red. "Never going to miss out on this again. You're mine, Tony."

Tony shivered at the possessiveness of those words, but it wasn't from fear. Instead, it was anticipation. He couldn't wait to experience every kind of pleasure and attentiveness Kellan had planned.

"I'm yours," Tony agreed on a whisper. "All yours."

"Yessss," Kellan hissed as he rubbed his hands all over Tony's torso for a moment as if mapping his skin. He touched his chest, his nipples, his abdominals, and his thighs. Finally, Kellan gently cradled Tony's balls while lightly rubbing his dick. With a feral grin, he warned, "If you don't move, I'll move you myself."

Having lost himself in Kellan's exquisite touch, Tony wasn't certain he had the ability to move. He whined as he rocked his hips a little, but the hard shaft in his ass didn't let him go far. Even knowing he needed to adjust his weight so he could get some leverage, Tony just couldn't seem to find the coordination. His vampire lover's touch was just too damn exquisite.

"Mmmm, I do love that I've melted your muscles, my beloved," Kellan rumbled, smug satisfaction thick in his tone. "Now, let me take care of you."

Then Kellan gripped Tony's hips and lifted, pulling him half off of his cock. A second later, he thrust into him. He did it over and over again, rutting into him swiftly.

Resting his palms on his vampire's chest, Tony held on for the ride. He clutched at his lover's strong frame, relishing every damn second of it. When Kellan found his prostate, he arched his back and cried out his ecstasy.

"Sssoooo gooood," Tony moaned out, feeling his balls pull tight.

"That's it, Tony," Kellan crooned. "Come for me. Paint my chest. Make me smell like you. Want it."

Tony figured he would feel embarrassed later at how swiftly he gave in to orgasm. Right then, however, he couldn't help himself. His balls and cock throbbed as his release surged through him, bliss blanking his senses.

Crying Kellan's name, Tony shuddered and shivered within his lover's grip. When the vampire urged him down to sprawl over him, he didn't even try to fight it. Then he felt Kellan's mouth at his neck.

For an instant, Tony tensed.

Except, the feel of Kellan licking over his skin immediately relaxed him. "That's the way," he purred into Tony's ear. "Relax while I claim you. All mine."

"Yours," Tony murmured back.

"Mine," Kellan repeated.

A second later, Kellan bit. His fangs popped through Tony's skin, causing the briefest flash of pain. It was immediately swallowed up by pleasure as tingles caused his skin to goose bump. The sensation shot straight to Tony's groin, and as Kellan sucked on his neck, it felt as if he were sucking his dick.

A few seconds later, Tony felt a second orgasm blindside him with bliss.

When Kellan eased his teeth from Tony's neck, it roused him from his cloud of endorphins. He smiled and hummed when the vampire licked over his skin, knowing he closed the wound. For some reason, even that felt fantastic.

Turning his head, Tony nuzzled Kellan's chest, drawing his lover's attention. "I'm sorry I was trying to fight this," Tony whispered the admission. "I was wrong."

"A shift in reality is difficult under the best of times," Kellan murmured back, his voice low and intimate. "And you were already exhausted and overwrought from caring for Shellie and dealing with her ex for months." He rubbed up and down Tony's back soothingly. "In truth, I feel blessed because I thought it would take longer."

"Well, I'm glad it didn't."

Tony's gaze fell upon the container of fruit and the can of whipping cream. With a smile, he gathered a bit of strength and eased back to an upright position. He could still feel Kellan's cock in his ass, even though it had begun to soften.

Wanting to change that, Tony grabbed the can and the container of fruit.

Kellan must have misunderstood his meaning, for he began to sit up. "Are you hungry?" He gripped Tony's hips and started to lift him. "We can relax and eat nude." Kellan waggled his eyebrows. "The others will scent that we're not available long before they get within eyesight."

"Stop moving," Tony ordered, slapping the container to Kellan's chest.

The vampire obeyed, probably more from surprise than because he didn't want to spill the open container.

"Tony?"

With a smirk, Tony replied, "Yes, I do believe I am hungry, but I'm not moving, yet, either."

Kellan arched one brow in silent question.

Placing the container near his knee, Tony picked up a slice of pineapple. "Did you know these are my favorite?" he asked as he poured a dollop of whipping cream onto it.

"No," Kellan admitted.

Pleased to hear the huskiness returning to Kellan's voice, Tony placed the slice onto his vampire's nipple. "Yup." He ignored the man's hiss, knowing the food wasn't *too* cold. Plus, it caused Kellan's nipple to bead, which lifted the fruit just a smidge.

"Tony?" Kellan whispered questioningly.

Tony took advantage. He dipped and licked over Kellan's nipple, taking the cream-covered pineapple with it. As Tony chewed, he hummed appreciatively, relishing the mixture of tangy and sweet.

"Fuck."

Enjoying the whine in Kellan's tone, Tony grabbed another piece of pineapple and prepared it. As he placed it on his lover's other nipple, he ground his ass against his vampire's groin. To Tony's delight, Kellan didn't try to stop him. He just rested his hands on Tony's thighs and massaged lightly.

As he ate several more slices off of Kellan's chest, satisfaction filled him upon feeling his lover's cock harden within him once more.

Chapter Twelve

Pain and pleasure swirled, becoming one.

Kellan couldn't remember the last time he'd allowed another to play with his body . . . just because. Except, this was his beloved, his one and only, his everything. He would always give Tony anything he wanted, if it was within his power.

And lying here while my beloved eats food off my chest is definitely within my power, even if my cock throbs so bad I'm afraid I'm going to blow again.

Watching Tony squirt a dollop of cream onto a slice of pineapple, Kellan's stomach trembled. He knew it was anticipation. There was just something so decadent in watching his lover eat off his chest.

Tony placed the slice on a new part of Kellan's torso, the cool of the fruit causing his skin to tingle in a way that caused both pleasure and pain. Watching Tony lick his lips sent a zing to Kellan's balls. Then he leaned over and stuck out his tongue.

For a few seconds, Tony played with the pineapple slice. He licked off a bit of the cream before nibbling on the edge of the fruit. After biting off a bit, he let the slice flop back to Kellan's chest. Humming, Tony chewed, pleasure and a hint of teasing filling his deep brown eyes.

After swallowing, Tony murmured appreciatively, "So delicious. How'd you get the perfect ripeness?"

Kellan had no idea how Tony could be coherent enough to talk because he was sure struggling. Still, he forced himself to answer. "Francois picks it out," he admitted. "Somehow, he knows."

Tony nodded, but he didn't comment. Instead, he grabbed another pineapple slice. That time, he poured the cream directly onto Kellan's nipple.

Groaning, Kellan shivered under the coolness of the whipping cream. A fresh wave of sparks cascaded through him as he felt Tony swipe the fruit slice across his covered nipple, scooping some up while tapping it at the same time. He panted harshly as he watched Tony pop it into his mouth, appearing completely pleased with himself.

Losing the battle with control, as soon as Tony swallowed, Kellan grabbed his beloved. Unmindful of the half-full bowl of fruit nearby, he rolled them. He ignored Tony's squeak even as his prick slipped partway out of his chute.

Kellan had Tony on his back within two seconds and his cock back deep in his body right after. "You are such a little minx," he rumbled as he began a slow rut. He adjusted his angle so he knew he only glanced his beloved's prostate ever-so-lightly. "Quite the tease."

Tony groaned and lifted his legs, wrapping them around Kellan's waist. "Loved that you let me," he admitted as he grabbed Kellan's forearms in his hands. "So much fun."

"Soon, I'm going to do the same to you," Kellan told Tony. With an eyebrow waggle, he told him, "I'm especially fond of peanut butter and honey."

To Kellan's delight, he felt a shiver work through his human's body. Grinning, he murmured, "You like that idea, don't you?" He teased a braid between his fingertips as he began to speed up his ruts. His need for relief in his cock and balls was beginning to get the better of him. "I look forward to more fun. But first."

Kellan cradled Tony's neck with one hand. With the other, he gripped his shoulder. Lowering his head, he captured his beloved's mouth. Kellan delved his tongue into Tony's mouth, tasting cream, pineapple, and something that was all his beloved.

Moaning, Kellan picked up his pace. He also adjusted his angle, making certain to peg his lover's prostate with each rut. As much as his balls cried for relief, Kellan needed Tony with him even more.

"Come, my beloved," Kellan demanded even as a surge of satisfaction flooded him that he could finally say that.

To Kellan's pleasure, and relief, Tony obeyed. His lover bucked beneath him, crying his name. As the heady aroma of Tony's pleasure flooded the air anew, Kellan felt his human's chute contract and release spastically around his length, yanking him over the edge with him.

Kellan was only too happy to go.

As Kellan shuddered above Tony, filling his human with his essence, he nuzzled his temple against his lover's. He hummed as bliss-inducing endorphins pinged through his system. Nothing had ever prepared him for the feeling of coupling with the other half of his soul.

My Tony. My beloved.

"Yeah, I'm yours," Tony slurred back, rubbing up and down Kellan's back.

Chuckling huskily, Kellan mumbled, "I didn't say that out loud."

"Yes, you did." Tony sounded a bit more with it, turning his head and frowning at him. "I heard you."

"Through our bond." Kellan couldn't believe how proud he was that it had formed so quickly. Except, upon seeing Tony's confused look, he realized he'd forgotten to explain. "Bonded vampires can speak with their beloveds telepathically."

"Really?"

Kellan nodded.

Tony's eyes narrowed. "You can't read my mind, can

you?"

Shaking his head, Kellan explained, "I can only hear things you project to me." Seeing Tony's confused expression, he added, "I'll help you with that. Teach you how it's done."

As a vampire, Kellan had an innate instinct on how to use his bond, but he knew that Tony wouldn't have that gift.

Before Tony could reply, Kellan's cell phone went off. Groaning, Kellan dropped his forehead onto his beloved's shoulder. Still, he began fumbling to the left, searching for his jeans.

"Can't you ignore it?"

As much as Kellan wished he could, he knew he couldn't. "That's Master Dante's private number," he explained. "He wouldn't be interrupting if there wasn't a damn good reason."

After all, his master knew he was out here trying to seduce his skittish human.

Tony nodded, hiding his look of disappointment, but Kellan could still detect it in his scent. Easing his softening prick free of his beloved, he grabbed his phone. He cast an apologetic look Tony's way even as he answered.

"Yes, Dante?"

"Is Tony with you?"

The fact that his master didn't greet him put Kellan on high alert. "Yes."

"Good. I need you both back here now." After a second of hesitation, Dante added, "Sheriff Diloan is here with an arrest warrant for Tony. Kidnapping."

"What the hell?" Kellan cried, jumping to his feet.

"Yes, I know it's bogus," Dante hissed into the phone. "But Officer Pedro Rodriguez from Detroit is accompanying him, and he's insisting." Chuckling coldly, he stated, "So far, Karina has kept Shellie's smell away from any area a cheetah could scent. I want them both to arrive together."

"Yes, Master. We'll be there in less than twenty."

"Good." With that, Dante disconnected the line.

Kellan dropped the phone on the blanket, noticing Tony was already dressing in a hurry. "Hear that?"

"Enough."

Nodding, Kellan started yanking on the essentials of his own clothing. "I heard you can ride. Gallop much?"

"I'll keep pace," Tony vowed.

Taking his beloved at his word, Kellan nodded. He skipped underwear, undershirt, and socks. Within seconds, he was slamming his bare feet into his boots. His phone went back into his belt holder, and his hat was on his head.

Kellan didn't know how Tony had done it, but he'd beaten him in dressing and already sat on his horse. Untying his own animal, he pointed the gelding toward home. With a bounce, Kellan was in the saddle, and they took off.

Even knowing his master needed him back asap, Kellan checked his horse's speed any time he noticed Tony appearing to struggle. They still made it back to the ranch within the twenty minutes he'd told his master. He rounded the barn so they approached from behind and wasn't surprised to spot Kase there waiting, ready to take their horses.

"Use the side door, Second," Kase offered. "The master has them in the upstairs study. Shellie and Karina are waiting in the family room." Then his eyes widened, and a grin stretched his lips. "And congratulations!"

Kellan couldn't help but smile. "Thank you."

As Kellan ushered Tony across the yard to the side of the ranch house, his beloved asked, "Why did he congratulate you?"

Ginning, Kellan winked. "He could smell the changes in our scents. He knows we bonded."

For a second, Tony didn't respond. Then he froze and gaped. "He can *smell* that we had sex?"

Sighing, Kellan nodded. "Yes." He tapped the side of his nose, reminding, "Paranormal noses. Remember?"

"Good grief," Tony muttered with a roll of his eyes. Grabbing Kellan's hand, he started them forward again as he declared, "We're going to have a deep discussion later. I'm tired of surprises."

"Of course, my beloved." Kellan would do the best he could to answer everything.

Slipping in through the side door, Kellan led the way through a mudroom and down a hallway. He followed his nose and knocked lightly on a side door to the family room. A second later, Karina opened the door and peered out at him.

Kellan typed a quick message to Dante, telling him that they were there. He didn't wait for his master to respond, knowing he would have things under control.

Heading up the stairs, Kellan took them to Dante's formal office where he met outsiders. The space was damn similar to his personal office, except it was at the top of the stairs rather than next to his and Ruth's bedroom. There was also a lack of actual files there, and the laptop was always kept empty of information.

After a single knock, Kellan opened the door. He nodded to Dante once, pleased and proud that he'd bonded. Seeing the flash of warmth in his master's eyes, he knew his friend was just as pleased for him.

"Ah, Kellan. Thank you for getting here so quickly," Dante greeted, rising from his seat behind his desk. "Please, come in."

Kellan led the way. A sweep of the office told him Sheriff Diloan sat in a chair in the lounging area of the office off to the right. With him was a man that Kellan didn't recognize. The fact that the scent of cat permeated the room told him the guy was Pedro.

On a nearby small sofa sat not only Monte, but also War in

human form. Monte's other beloved, Xerxes, was at the side-board. He appeared to be in the process of refreshing drinks.

War scented the air, then grinned broadly. Xerxes paused and gasped. He smiled widely and gave Kellan two thumbs up.

Tony groaned as he followed him inside, mumbling, "Great. Everyone can smell it. You're in so much trouble, Kel."

Kellan couldn't wait to see what Tony thought trouble was, but he refrained from saying that.

"That's him," Pedro declared, interrupting the silence. Standing, he pointed at Tony. "Arrest him."

"Why are you trying to arrest Tony, Pedro," Shellie de-manded, following them into the room. Karina was on her heels, slipping an arm around her waist as soon as she could. Shellie sure looked cozy there as she frowned at Pedro and asked, "Is this more of Barry's nonsense?"

Pedro narrowed his gaze as he frowned at them all. Instead of answering them, he focused on the sheriff. "Well, Sheriff Diloan? What are you waiting for?"

Sheriff Diloan took the drink from Xerxes and thanked him. After taking a sip of the clear beverage—from the lack of scent, Kellan guessed it was water—he focused on Shellie. "It seems someone is under the impression that you've been kid-napped, Shellie."

Shellie barked a laugh as she rolled her eyes. "God, that sounds like Barry's shenanigans." Sighing dramatically, she continued, "He's my ex-husband, and he's pissed that I left him for someone else." Shellie indicated Karina. "Now he's trying to cause enough chaos in the life of me and my friends that I'll sign over custody of my son to him." She leveled a hard look on Pedro. "You go back to Detroit and tell Barry that it will *never* happen."

The sheriff turned to Pedro. "Well, I'm afraid you have

your answer. Miss Desprow has not been kidnapped." He smiled at Pedro. "I'm certain you're happy to confirm that no crime has been committed. I'll file the necessary paperwork to cancel the kidnapping charges as soon as I get back to the office."

"You can't do that," Pedro declared. "There were witnesses. There were—"

"I have the only witness who matters standing right in front of me," the sheriff cut in. Resting his hand on his hip, he stated, "Look. It's obvious to me that this is a matter of a disgruntled ex-husband. I don't look too kindly on someone trying to besmirch the character of another for selfish reasons in my town." Narrowing his eyes, Sheriff Diloan stated gruffly, "I suggest you and your people remember that before returning with bogus claims."

"I'll escort him out," War claimed, rising to his feet. With a smirk, he added, "Don't worry, Sheriff. I'll make certain he understands your stance."

A second later, War grabbed Pedro's arm and hauled the cat shifter out of the room, taking the sudden scent of fear with him.

Kellan knew the horseman had that effect on people sometimes.

"Thank you, Sheriff," Dante stated. "I appreciate your patience."

Sheriff John Diloan snorted as he returned to his chair. "I'll take that gin now, Xerxes," he stated before focusing on Dante. "Ever since you and your people have started finding your beloveds, problems have been rolling into town."

The vampire master shrugged. "What can I say? Fate brings couples together when they need each other most."

John hummed. "Makes sense." Then he took the drink from Xerxes, thanking him.

Dante focused on Kellan and smiled. "That won't be the

end of it," he warned. Then he inhaled deeply and narrowed his eyes. "But the rest can wait until you and your beloved have showered." Dante waved his hand dismissively. Just as Kellan was following Tony out the door, his master called, "Congratulations to you both."

Spotting Tony's glare, Kellan knew he was going to be paying for his oversight . . . and he couldn't wait for every blissful second of it.

Yeah. Life is good.

YOU MAY ALSO ENJOY THE FOLLOWING FROM EXTASY BOOKS INC:

Winning the Survivalist
Charlie Richards

Excerpt

While wiping his damp fingertips on the leg of his jeans, Markus heard his microphone chirp to life. "This is dispatch. Come in, Deputy Reussmin."

Recognizing Michelle Laraby's voice, Markus fought the urge to roll his eyes. Only their station's receptionist could make it sound as if contacting him was beneath her while over the radio. He sometimes wondered if she had a stick up her ass all the time, or if it was just because she was working with a bunch of dominant males that she decided she had to a be, well . . . a bitch. Markus wasn't certain. Michelle had been that way since the day he was hired on part time. He loved that he'd been able to join full time two years prior.

Maybe she just needs to get laid.

Markus pressed the transmit button on his microphone and replied, "This is Deputy Reussmin. Go ahead, dispatch."

"I've received three reports of smoke about a mile west of Hormel Peak trailhead. There's no camping in there," Michelle pointed out needlessly.

Markus already knew that.

Before Markus could reply, Michelle continued, "Sheriff Parkinson wants you to check it out."

"I'll be back at my vehicle in five minutes, dispatch," Markus replied, starting that way with ground-eating strides. "I'll be on the road shortly. How long ago were the reports?"

He didn't ask why it had taken three of them before the sheriff had decided to check it. Sheriff Blake Parkinson was getting on in years, but he kept putting off retirement because he feared a fag would replace him.

Not that Blake had actually said that in front of anyone. Markus had happened to overhear it just the prior week. Blake had been on the phone, and his door had been cracked open—probably by accident.

Mental note, tell Declan about it.

Markus knew Declan would find a way to get a gay-friendly person in office. Hell, it would probably end up being a shifter. Markus wondered if it would end up being one of the detectives.

"The first source wasn't credible. The second source said the fire faded as they watched," Michelle told him, answering his unspoken curiosity. "It wasn't until we received a call from Ranger Holsteen that Sheriff Parkinson decided there may be something to it."

Markus did roll his eyes then. Ranger Holsteen was actually Beta Dixon Holsteen, second-in-command of their wolf pack. If he'd noticed a fire, then there had to be some problem out there.

I wonder why the rangers aren't checking it then.

Unable to contain his curiosity a second time, Markus asked just that.

Michelle's sniff actually came through the line. "Evidently, they're on a call about an injured hiker. They won't have anyone available for at least three hours, so they asked us to check it."

"Got it." As Markus approached his vehicle, he used his

fob to unlock it. "I'm on it. I'll report back as soon as I can."

Markus slid behind the wheel before firing it up. Once he'd pulled the belt around himself, he checked his mirrors and eased out of the parking lot. Heading north out of town, Markus wondered what he would find.

While it was still technically the rainy season, a lightning strike could still start a forest fire. There was enough snow on the ground that it would fizzle swiftly, though. If several people saw it, there was a possibility of a poacher camping out there.

It had been years, but that didn't mean it was out of the realm of possibility. As wolf shifters, they patrolled their territory regularly, but they controlled a big area. Someone could have slipped through.

"If it is a poacher, I'll cross that bridge when I get to it," Markus murmured to himself.

As Markus drove deeper into the mountains, he noticed patches of snow increasing. His vehicle's temperature gage ticked lower and lower. By the time he reached the area he needed, the truck's thermometer told him it was forty-seven degrees outside.

"Damn," Markus muttered. "If it really is a poacher, they're diehard about it."

Markus hoped he didn't find anyone.

Driving slowly away from the Hormel Peak trailhead parking area, heading west, Markus kept sweeping over the tops of the trees. He'd traveled nearly two miles along the winding road and was beginning to think it was a bogus call or the fire was already out. Except, that didn't seem like something his pack beta would do or make a mistake about.

With his faith in his pack beta driving him onward, Markus kept looking. He stopped after five miles and frowned. Turning this way and that in his seat, he tried to decide if he should turn around and make another pass or call Dixon to see if he could get a more specific location.

As much as he was loath to interrupt his beta while in the

middle of a call, Markus didn't know if he was in the right area. He didn't really have faith in Sheriff Parkinson or Michelle to get their information right. The pair had been at the job so long, in a small town with very little crime, that they'd grown more than a little lax.

Part of that problem might be the fact that most of the crime was pack related, so they hid it from the pair.

Just as Markus picked up his phone, a hint of gray to his left caught his attention. He rolled down his window, bracing himself against the cold air. Lifting his shades, he squinted as he looked over the pine treetops.

There, in the distance, was a thin wisp of smoke.

"Damn," Markus mumbled. "There's not supposed to be anything out there. It's state park property."

Rolling up his window, Markus pulled his vehicle onto the shoulder at the first safe place he found. He turned in his seat and grabbed his heavy sheriff's coat from the backseat. After exiting his truck, he pulled on the thick fabric and zipped it.

Markus radioed in that he'd spotted the smoke and the mile marker where he'd roughly left his truck. Then he started into the forest.

As a wolf shifter, Markus didn't feel the cold quite as intensely as a human would. Hiking through the chilly mid-morning air, he was damn grateful for that. He didn't envy any human trying to camp in the mountains of Colorado in the spring.

Maybe it's a paranormal.

The random thought flitted through his brain. He supposed it was a possibility. That meant whoever it was would probably be on the run from someone.

"Let's not jump to conclusions," Markus muttered.

His imagination was getting away from him.

As much as Markus tried to be quiet, his boots crunched on the dead leaves, spots of snow, and wet branches littering the ground. He slowly weaved his way through the pines, keeping in the general direction he'd spotted the smoke. When his sensitive shifter nose picked up the hint of burning timber, Markus knew he was getting close.

Finally, Markus ran across a deer trail heading in the right direction and began to follow it. He'd been on it for less than ten minutes when a small, ten-by-fifteen-foot clearing opened up before him. Seeing the set up within, he froze, his hand instinctively lowering to his revolver.

There was a tent tucked under the bows of a pine on the right, covered in a waterproof tarp. Bows lined the base and bottom, providing extra warmth. A fire pit lined with rocks was five feet in front of the tent's opening. Someone had even fashioned a make-shift cover over it using sticks lashed together with twine and bark.

Markus felt the hairs on the back of his neck lift, the sensation telling him that he was being watched. Inhaling slowly, he swept his gaze over the area once more, searching. He didn't see anyone.

Except, the scent called to him on a primitive level he'd never before experienced. His blood heated in his veins, and his wolf urged at him to track down the source.

Shock flooded him as realization set in.

Somewhere in these woods, hiding from me, is my mate. Just what the fuck could he be doing out here?

And where is he?

About the Author

Charlie started writing fantasy when she was eight, and after stumbling onto her first erotic romance at age nineteen, she realized her true calling. She now focuses on writing gay erotic romance, normally of the paranormal variety, with heroes of all kinds. With the help and support of her husband, Charlie finally fulfilled one of her life-long goals . . . move to acreage with her horses. You can often find her curled up with her laptop and a cup of tea or glass of wine, creating her next adventure. Charlie enjoys exploring the mountains of her new Oregon home on horseback, 4-wheeler, or motorcycle.

She can be reached at ch.richards2010@yahoo.com
Or visit her at www.charlie-richards.com